"Hugh Ashton does a fantastic job of continuing the Sherlock Holmes legacy in the true tradition and style of Sir Arthur Conan Doyle."

"The writing style completely recreates the work of Sir Arthur Conan Doyle and provides a perfect continuation of the famous adventures of the great detective. I plan to read all of these books, they are like finding treasure thought lost for many years."

"...the characters, from Holmes and Watson to Lestrade and all the minor characters appearing in the stories, are masterfully rendered in a way that is both faithful to the original and at the same time subtly innovative."

"Unlike Sir Arthur Conan Doyle, who got tired of his logical creation, Sherlock Holmes, Hugh Ashton clearly loves the character and his traits. I kept thinking that I was reading a more clever, sharper, wittier, just generally better writer, doing Conan Doyle like it should have been done."

"There is the feel of the stratified society, the scent of coal smoke in your nose, and the slightly foggy streets of 19th century London radiate around you as you read these stories... These are thoroughly enjoyable and completely authentic in feel and atmosphere, and we can almost hear Holmes whispering, ' Come, now; the game's afoot...and do bring your revolver with you.' "

FURTHER NOTES
FROM THE DISPATCH-BOX
OF
JOHN H. WATSON MD

Further Notes from The Dispatch-Box of
John H. Watson MD:
More Untold Adventures of Sherlock Holmes

Hugh Ashton

ISBN-10: 0615806570
ISBN-13: 978-0615806570

Published by Inknbeans Press, 2013

www.inknbeans.com

www.221BeanBakerStreet.info

Inknbeans Press, 25060 Hancock Avenue Bldg 103 Suite 458, Murrieta CA 92562, USA

DEDICATION

O my father, David Ashton.

FOREWORD BY
PHILIP C. EYSTER, D.MIN.

 HEN I was about 10 years old, I received " The Canon". Up until that time, the only " Canon" with which I was familiar was the Bible. For a young boy, this book of over a thousand pages and no pictures presented a daunting assignment. Yet I dug in and found myself enthralled with each story, and completed the book in a year or so. That volume followed me to college, where my roommate and I had a standing appointment each Saturday evening to read aloud one story over a late night pizza.

It wasn't until I had read The Canon through four or five times that I realised I needed more. There must be something more. These were the days before the internet, and I wasn't in contact with other fans and had never heard the word " pastiche". Finally, I came across *The Exploits of Sherlock Holmes* by Adrian Conan Doyle and John Dickson Carr published in 1955. I was back in business with 12 " new" stories about my hero.

In the mid 1980s I began to travel internationally for my work on a regular basis, usually every other month. These travels always took me through London, where I would build in a day to walk up and down Charing Cross Road, entering every used bookshop, looking for " more". I was often rewarded with a new book full of more tales, some good and some not so good.

Somewhere along the way, my interest turned into an obsession, I simply had to have " more". It was at this point that I embarked on a quest for the " perfect pastiche". That story, which, if placed alongside the originals, would never be recognized or out of place.

Since the 1890s Doyle's detective has been immortalized in both parody and pastiche. In the last 20 years the genre has gone " viral". The last three years have seen the advent of two major motion pictures, a BBC production in the UK, and another programme in the US placing Holmes in contemporary New York City. It might be safe to say that Sherlock Holmes has never been more popular. There are estimated to be over 10,000 novels and short stories about the man from Baker Street. With such a volume of material, it becomes clear that the average Sherlockian can not read everything. One must discriminate and find those works that yield the most enjoyment. How do you like your Holmes ? Confidently extracting the truth from late 19th century murderers, or battling Dracula and extraterrestrials ?

Over the past 30 years, I've learned that some authors either by design, default, or disability write tales that only bear a passing resemblance to the originals. Yet for my taste, I want my Holmes and Watson to live forever with the same personalities, foibles, idiosyncrasies, and vocabulary.

While many make a valiant attempt at a faithful pastiche, I found that very few are able to carry it off. And distinguishing the good from the mediocre is akin to the difference between art and pornography; it's hard to define, but you know it when you see it.

Into this rarified air comes Hugh Ashton with his newly discovered Dispatch and Deed Boxes. I had only read a few pages of his initial story, when I knew that Mr. Ashton has not only the skill but also the deep-felt desire to add faithfully to the canon the same Sherlock as came from the pen of Arthur Conan Doyle over 100 years ago.

Mr. Ashton has said that " Developing the style is relatively easy, and finding a crime, and planting the clues that allow Holmes to solve the crime, not too hard".

To which, in response, I would offer Hugh's own dialogue between Holmes and Watson after Sherlock displays his expertise at deducing details of a client's life before ever meeting them. Watson says, " You make it sound absurdly simple." Holmes replies, " It is indeed absurdly simple, and yet I seem to be the only man in London—nay, in the whole kingdom—who seems capable of the feat".

Based on the number of authors who try and the few that succeed, Hugh Ashton makes something incredibly difficult look easy, and he " seems to be the only man in the whole kingdom capable of the feat."

So sit down, and be transformed back into the age of gaslights and gasogenes. Where Queen Victoria rules the realm and the king of consulting detectives paces the sitting room floor, stopping every so often to look out the window for the arrival of another poor soul in trouble.

This volume you hold in your hand gives us the Holmes of history. Hugh tackles the *Abernetty Horror* mentioned by Watson in the *Six Napoleons*, and is famous for the pairing of parsley and butter. Mr. Ashton then authors a longer substantive tale of *The Finsbury House*, based on Holmes' passing reference in *The Norwood Builder* to " the Dutch steamship *Friesland*" which does indeed nearly cost them both their lives.

Ashton then lightens up the mood in *The Affair of the Archdeacon*, before finishing this volume with *The Victor Lynch Forgery* case, an early tale as told through the pen of Inspector Lestrade of Scotland Yard and referred to in *A Study in Scarlet* and *The Sussex Vampire*.

With these four new stories, Hugh Ashton's pen provides the details of cases mentioned but never clarified. And I feel confident in labeling each story as " The Perfect Pastiche".

" *Tolle Lege*" (St. Augustine) " Take up and read".

Dr. Philip C. Eyster
Consulting Sherlockian
Maine, USA

EDITOR'S NOTES
BY HUGH ASHTON

 AM STILL WORKING my way through the second box deposited so long ago by the friend and biographer of Sherlock Holmes, Doctor John Watson in the vaults of the now defunct Cox & Co. of Charing Cross.

How many more boxes could there be? I was sure that the box I entitled the "deed box" and from which I took my first three collections and the novel *The Darlington Substitution* was the one mentioned in *Thor Bridge*, but I was mistaken. I have yet to be convinced that this present box, the "dispatch-box", is the last set of Dr. Watson's memoirs to be discovered. Who knows what other literary treasures lie at the bottom of the vault of the bank that took over Cox's business. Maybe they will include not only those which shed more light on Sherlock Holmes, but also others which will add to our knowledge of other famous figures of the past?

Out of this "dispatch-box" collection, I have selected four accounts for this collection, all of which have been mentioned by Watson in those accounts that he wrote and published through his agent, Sir Arthur Conan Doyle.

The first of these is the *Abernetty Horror*. An intriguing story, where the discovery of the guilty parties hinges on a small detail which would be overlooked by almost everyone, but failed to escape the notice of Sherlock Holmes.

The story of *Finsbury House* was untitled by Watson, and I have taken the liberty of giving it its present name, based on the location where most of the misdeeds described therein took place. For Holmes and Watson, these events were connected with the steamship *Friesland*, which would have impressed itself on their memory more forcibly, as a result of the emotional trauma they suffered on board (if I may be permitted a lapse into 20th-century psychology).

By contrast, the *Affair of the Archdeacon* (also untitled by Watson) appeared to me to be sufficiently amusing and to provide enough of a contrast to the previous adventure to warrant its inclusion here.

As I mentioned in the previous compilation of Holmes' adventures collected from this box, *Notes from the Dispatch-Box of John H. Watson MD*, this collection of papers seems to be a more heterogeneous and eclectic collection of records. The last collection contained the villain John Clay's account of his life. Here we see a case, mentioned in passing by Holmes in *The Sussex Vampire*, which is not told by Watson, but by a professional policeman—the celebrated Inspector Lestrade. We see here the account of one of the first (if not the first) of Holmes' cases as a consulting detective, and we gain an insight into the early Holmes and his relationship with the police.

There well may be other such accounts from outside the Holmes-Watson partnership which are waiting to be discovered, and these will no doubt throw further light on the adventures of the great sleuth, though whether they will corroborate or contradict Dr. Watson's accounts has yet to be determined.

I am deeply gratified also by the responses of my readers to the previous stories of Sherlock Holmes and John Watson that I have published. Rest assured that this collection is not the last of its kind.

The game continues to be afoot, and we have not yet reached the bottom of the last box.

ACKNOWLEDGEMENTS

ANY THANKS TO ALL who have assisted in making this book what it is. No writer is an island—and I am no exception.

Many thanks to Dr. Philip C. Eyster, the Maine-based consulting Sherlockian, for his foreword to this volume. While reading the stories, he has made one or two comments and suggestions that I have gratefully accepted and incorporated.

Jo, the Boss Bean at Inknbeans Press, has continued to provide support and help throughout the production of this and all the other books, including during a time of great emotional stress. Thank you. A writer could have no better editor, publisher—and friend.

Yoshiko, my wife, who has come to live in Baker-street through her reading of the original canon in Japanese. She now has some more understanding of what I am trying to achieve and is not as bemused by Sherlock as she was.

CONTENTS

FURTHER NOTES
FROM THE DISPATCH-BOX
OF
JOHN H. WATSON MD

MORE UNTOLD ADVENTURES OF
SHERLOCK HOLMES

AS DISCOVERED BY
HUGH ASHTON

SHERLOCK HOLMES AND THE
ABERNETTY HORROR

EDITOR'S NOTE

This adventure is one that is mentioned in The Six Napoleons. *Holmes tells Watson, " You will remember, Watson, how the dreadful business of the Abernetty family was first brought to my notice by the depth which the parsley had sunk into the butter on a hot day".*

He refers to this as one of his " most classic cases", and it has been a matter of some disappointment to Sherlockians that Watson never published the case, though it must, from the way that Holmes refers to it, have been familiar to him.

It was, therefore, with an extreme sense of pleasure that the stack of papers headed Abernetty (the name of a village, not a family, according to Watson, though it would appear that it is a pseudonym, since I have been unable to locate it in any gazetteer) came to light in the dispatch-box. It is indeed a classic case, showing Holmes' mastery of observation and of human nature at their best.

T WAS ONE OF THE HOTTEST SUMMERS that I can remember when Sherlock Holmes and I made our way to a coastal village in Wales to escape the heat of London. Holmes had expressed himself to be loath to leave the capital, claiming that the cool of the Reading Room in the British Museum was sufficient for his needs, but I insisted that we should spend at least a few days out of the stink of the metropolis.

The small fishing village of Abernetty where we had taken rooms was hardly conducive to putting Holmes in a good mood. On his rare trips away from London, he was usually able to find congenial company in the form of the local gentry, or of the local parson or priest. In this particular instance, however, the nearest country seat, Abernetty Hall, despite its name, was only reachable by a tramp of some five miles over rough country. From what we had heard, the local squire would not in any case have presented himself as a suitable candidate for Holmes' companionship. Lacking a church, the village of Abernetty nevertheless possessed two chapels of Nonconformist denominations, whose ministers, though doubtless good enough fellows in their own way, likewise lacked the capacity for intellectual stimulation which Holmes craved.

We were staying at the house of a Mrs. Williams, and though the fare that she provided for us could in no way be described as Epicurean, or the accommodation as being luxurious, we were comfortable. We were the only guests in the house, but some two days after we arrived in the village, the house next to ours, occupied by a family of fishermen, named Griffiths, entertained a visitor from the Midlands.

Holmes was sitting by the window of the drawing room as the new visitor arrived in the trap which had brought him, as it had conveyed us, from Aberystwyth station. " What do you make of him, Watson ? " he asked me.

" He is unused to this kind of life," I laughed. " His boots tell me that." Indeed, the patent leather boots that our new neighbour was wearing seemed singularly inappropriate.

" Maybe his trunks will contain some more suitable footwear," Holmes answered me. " Anything else ? "

" I see very little to tell me any more."

" On the contrary, my dear Watson, you see everything that I see, but you fail to draw the appropriate conclusions from your observations. For example, I see that Mr. Fuller is a native of Wolverhampton. He is a successful

businessman, engaged in the manufacture of certain cook-
ing utensils. He is of a somewhat parsimonious disposition, and despite his rather unprepossessing appearance,
considers himself to be something of a ladies' man. He
is, of course, a bachelor and tends to overindulge in what
I fear our good neighbour Mrs. Griffiths would describe as
'the demon alcohol'. I must confess that I am more than
a little surprised that he has chosen this rather out of the
way spot for his holidays. I would rather have expected
him to take up temporary residence in a rather more fashionable watering place."

By this time, I was becoming accustomed to the deductions that my friend produced following his observations of
strangers, and I was able to follow his reasoning on most
of them, even though I was unable to initiate them myself.
" One of his boxes certainly bears the name of Fuller and
Co., and a description of the firm on it. From this I can
see that he almost certainly comes from Wolverhampton,
but how do you know that this is Mr. Fuller in person ? "

" It is obvious, from the rather overbearing nature and
air of command that he exhibits. This particular bearing
is common to self-made proprietors of a business."

" Very good. In which case, his parsimonious disposition can be explained by the fact that he is using one of his
firm's packing cases to transport his personal effects, rather than spending money on luggage. I agree that there is
a certain indefinable something that marks him as a single man, and the boots that we remarked earlier, together
with the overly ornate floral arrangement in his buttonhole, mark him as something of a dandy, and hence as a
man with a roving eye. But I still do not see the drink
that you mentioned as a part of his character."

" That was the simplest of them all," Holmes answered

me. " Surely the outline of his hip flask in his pocket was obvious when he descended from the trap ? If a man cannot live without drink within easy reach for the relatively short time that it takes to come here from Aberystwyth station, we may assume that alcohol may be deemed a necessary adjunct to his existence. However, you have followed my reasoning on all the other points. It is simply a matter of adding one's experience to one's observations."

" You make it sound absurdly simple."

" It is indeed absurdly simple, and yet I seem to be the only man in London—nay, in the whole kingdom—who seems capable of the feat."

I laughed at Holmes' pretensions. " You may be thankful that this is the case, for if it were otherwise, you might be bereft of a profession. Do we introduce ourselves to this Mr. Fuller, once he is settled ? "

" You may do so if you wish, but I fear that he will prove very poor company."

OLMES' PREDICTION was proved correct. Though I took the trouble to make myself known to Mr. Fuller, by the expedient of leaving my card at the Griffiths house, and though he returned the call the next morning, it seemed that we had little in common, and the subjects of which he spoke were either of little interest to me, or, containing as they did thinly veiled references to his experiences with the fair sex, were distasteful to me. It did seem indeed that Holmes' judgement of his character was correct. When not speaking of his manufactory and the business associated with it, Fuller's sole interest seemed to be the pursuit, and if I understood him correctly, the seduction, of as many young women as possible.

I heard him with barely suppressed anger. Such a man was far from being the type that I would choose as a companion, and I was thankful that Holmes was absent on one of his long walks along the shore, for though he could in no way be termed a romantic, his attitude towards women was almost invariably one of courtesy and chivalry. At the earliest possible opportunity, I contrived to have Fuller leave the house, though it appeared to me that he wished to continue the conversation longer.

When Holmes returned, I recounted the events of the morning to him.

" Even allowing for the exaggeration which is common among men of that type," he remarked, " it would seem wise for our neighbour Mrs. Griffiths to keep a close eye on her daughter."

I agreed. Young Gwen Griffiths, the daughter, was a fine figure of Welsh womanhood, and would undoubtedly attract the attentions of one such as Fuller. " She has three strapping brothers to protect her honour," I reminded him. Mrs. Griffiths, whose husband had perished at sea, as we had been told, kept the house with her three sons who carried on their father's trade as fishermen, and the youngest of the family, young Gwen.

Once again, Holmes proved himself to be a prophet. It was only the day after my conversation with Fuller that I observed him in conversation with the fair daughter of our neighbour. She appeared to be agitated, and he had caught hold of her sleeve, seemingly detaining her against her will. As I rounded the corner of the street where I beheld them, he caught sight of me, and immediately released her from his grip.

" A very good day to you, Watson ! " he sang out, in his unpleasing Midland accent.

It would have been churlish of me to cut him altogether, but I merely grunted a noncommittal reply and proceeded without speaking to him further. I turned into the lane that led to the tavern where I had been accustomed to refresh myself in company with the local villagers from time to time, and realised that I was being followed. I stopped and turned to behold David Griffiths, the youngest brother of young Gwen, who now hailed me.

" That man is no friend of yours, then, sir ? " he enquired of me, in a slightly aggressive tone of voice.

" By no means. The kind of behaviour that I just witnessed fills me with disgust, and I can tell you in all honesty that if he had not released your sister when he did, I would have used the strongest possible methods to make him do so."

A smile spread over his face. " I'm very pleased to hear you say that, sir," he told me in that curious Welsh sing-song accent. Me and my brothers would be very much obliged to you, sir, if you and the other gentleman staying next door would be good enough to keep an eye on Gwen. My brothers and I are out in the boat all the day, and with no man in the house, there's no knowing what might be going on."

" I am sure that I and my friend will be happy to do as you say. By the way, why are you not in the boat with your brothers today ? "

" I twisted my shoulder yesterday hauling in the net, and Owen and Gareth told me that today they could manage without me. Would you be going to the Dragon, sir ? Because if you are, I would like to express my thanks to you, if you understand my meaning."

I was happy to accept his invitation, and we made our way to the tavern, talking as we did so. I discovered several things about young Griffiths and his family. As we had been told, his father had drowned, tragically within sight of land, but the sea had been too rough for any attempt at a rescue. The three boys and their sister were left to fend for themselves, and support their mother, with the eldest of the boys being a mere seventeen years of age when he was orphaned. On our arrival at the Dragon, I waved aside his intention of purchasing my drink, and instead " stood a round" is the phrase has it, for him and the other occupants of the bar. This was much appreciated, and a place was made for me in the circle. I spent the best part of a happy hour listening to tales of life in the village, which held my interest, although the protagonists were unknown to me.

On my return to the Williams household, I informed Holmes of what had happened, including some details of the local gossip. " And our beauteous neighbour of next door," I concluded, " while not formally betrothed to the man generally reckoned to be the strongest in the village, a Mr. Dai Edwards who is a fisherman also, is generally reckoned to be attached to him and he to her. If our Mr. Fuller decides to pay her any attention, the general opinion of the taproom in the Dragon is that he would do best to leave the village before Mr. Edwards' boat returns to harbour. And of course, that is to say nothing of the three Williams brothers, who likewise seen pledged to defend the honour of their sister."

Holmes threw back his head and laughed heartily. " Good old Watson. I have my own methods of obtaining information, but I have to confess that in matters like these you have an uncanny knack of discovering the most trivial of details in a very short space of time. But I think that you are right to have made your promise to the Williams lad as regards keeping a watchful eye on Fuller. It is hard for me to be sure, since I am without my usual methods of verifying my information, but I am reasonably certain that this is a man who was acquitted, on evidence that I can only describe as dubious, in an embezzlement case a few years ago. My feeling is that we have a bad character as our neighbour, and even without the Williams girl, his presence here would add interest to an otherwise deathly dull community."

What Holmes described as " interest" is what most of the law-abiding world would describe as " crime". It must be admitted, though, that however congenial I had found the company of David Griffiths and his companions, and however beautiful the dramatic scenery of this part of Wales, there was a large part of me that agreed with Holmes' characterisation of the village, and I began to wonder whether we would not have been better served by a stay at Brighton or Eastbourne or some other fashionable watering place.

In the event, though, it was only a matter of a day before Holmes found something of interest to him—that is to say, before a crime requiring his extraordinary skills occurred.

We were sitting down to our evening meal, which Mrs. Williams termed " tea" (and indeed, a large brown pot filled with that beverage was placed in the centre of our table along with a ham salad, for it had been an unseasonably warm day, and our hostess had expressed her opinion, with which we concurred, that a hot meal in the evening would be unwelcome, bread, butter, and home-made cakes) when Mrs. Griffiths burst in, her face ashen.

" He's dead ! " she shrieked. " He's sitting there at the table, in a pool of his own blood ! "

Holmes, who had risen to his feet at her first words, gently took her by the arm and led her to a chair where she sat, shaking in obvious terror.

" Now then," he said softly to her. " Who is dead ? Is this one of your sons ? "

The terrified woman looked up at Holmes, her face wet with tears. " Oh no, sir, it's not one of my boys. It's that Mr. Fuller, the paying guest. He's dead," she repeated, and burst into hysterical sobbing. I moved to be near the woman, and placed a hand on her shoulder.

" Come now," I said in my most gentle tones. " You must tell us more."

The wretched woman broke down again, and dabbed at her eyes with a handkerchief. At length she spoke, but I was unable to catch the words. I looked at Holmes questioningly, but he too shook his head.

" She is speaking in Welsh, a language I have yet to master," he told me.

Our hostess answered her in the same language, and she started to speak in English.

" It was half an hour ago that I found him. I know it was half past five because the grandfather clock was just striking when I opened the door. I was bringing him his second pot of tea, because he liked his tea. And there he was, just sitting there, covered in blood, and the blood still dripping from him, drip, drip, drip, onto the best parlour carpet. I'll never be able to look at that carpet again," and once again she burst into sobs.

" Shall I call Constable Evans ? " Mrs. Williams asked Holmes.

" I think we had all better view the scene," he replied.

At the sound of his words, our visitor's hysterical sobs grew louder. " Oh no, sir. I'm not going in that room again. Not with him sitting there dead in his blood like that."

" Very good, Mrs. Griffiths," my friend said to her. " No one can force you to go in there. But you must tell us what happened as clearly as possible."

She wiped her eyes and looked up at him. " I took in his tea, and set it out on the table and then called him down to it, sir," she began.

" At what time was this ? " asked Holmes, who by now had pulled out his ever-present notebook, and was writing in it.

" I called him down to his tea at a twenty past five or a little after. It was the same sort of thing as you gentlemen were going to eat. A nice bit of ham from one of Morgan's pigs, a few bits of green and some bread and butter with some of my tea bread. And I'd made a good strong pot of tea to go with it all. Well, sir, he came down and went into the room. I came from the kitchen with the teapot, and like I say, the grandfather clock was just striking when I opened the door and I saw him there. I don't know quite what I did, but the next thing I knew was that my three boys were standing round me. I was lying on the floor, and I suppose I must have fainted away. My boys told me that they had come straight from the harbour, where they had come in from fishing on their boat and they had just discovered me lying on the floor there."

" What time was this ? "

" Just before I came here, sir."

" Let us say ten minutes past six, then," said Holmes, pulling out his watch and making a note of the time. " So you had been unconscious for about forty minutes." He paused, as if in thought. " Tell me," he said suddenly, " where was the teapot when you woke up ? "

Our visitor's face creased in thought. " I can't rightly say. That is to say, I don't know."

" May I ask where your daughter was while all these events were taking place ? "

It may have been my imagination, but it seemed to me that a guilty look passed across her face before she answered us. " She had gone out earlier that afternoon. She hasn't returned yet."

" Very well. Mrs. Williams," he addressed our landlady. " Please make Mrs. Griffiths comfortable, and when you feel she is settled, inform the constable of these events. Dr. Watson and I will step next door, and examine the scene."

All three of the Griffiths sons were standing outside the door of the house as we approached. David, the youngest, with whom I had spent some time in the Dragon, spoke to us first.

" I think you are too late, Doctor," he addressed me. " He's dead, if ever I saw a dead man."

" I am sure you are right, but I can assure you that my interest in this is not simply one of idle curiosity."

" Shouldn't you wait until the police arrive ? " one of the other brothers asked us.

Sherlock Holmes answered him. " In cases like this, I have found that the sooner these incidents are investigated, the more evidence remains to solve the case."

" You mean that you have done this sort of thing before ? " asked David Griffiths.

I answered for my friend. " Maybe you have heard of Sherlock Holmes ? " The three brothers nodded. " This is he."

The three looked at each other, and I saw what appeared to be a glance of dismay pass between them. " I still think you should wait for the police," said the one who had pre-viously expressed his opinion on that matter.

" I can assure you," Holmes told him in his most au-thoritative manner, " that the police will welcome my help in this investigation. If you gentlemen wish to assist, you can do so best by preventing anyone other than the po-lice from entering this house." Again a glance seem to be passed between the brothers, but they made no attempt to prevent us entering the house.

The interior of the house seemed to be unreasonably warm, and I found myself perspiring slightly as we reached the door of the fatal chamber. As we had been told, Full-er was sitting in his chair at the table, with his neck and chest covered in blood, which had splashed onto the table in places, and had dripped onto the carpet.

" It is no wonder that she said she could never use that carpet again," I remarked, shuddering.

" I am sure that our impressions, as well as those of the Griffiths family, are correct," Holmes answered me, " but if you will have the goodness to confirm that life is indeed ex-tinct, then I would be grateful."

I was thankful that my service in India had blunted my feelings at the sight of violent death—a sight which, I was well aware, had an effect even on some members of my profession. Sherlock Holmes, for his part, appeared to have nerves of steel where this sort of thing was concerned, and the sight of a bloody corpse seemed to affect him little more than the sight of a roast chicken on his dinner plate. I could detect no signs of life in this case, and reported as much.

" I know this is stretching your professional judgement to the limit, Watson, but would you be prepared to give any estimate as to the time of death ? "

" I think that the excessively warm atmosphere prevents me from giving any definite opinion on the matter, and I can only say that death has almost certainly occurred within the last hour or two. I am sorry not to be able to give any more precise an opinion than that."

" I feared as much," he replied. Moving to my side, he took the hand of the corpse, and flexed the wrist gently. The meal, set in front of the dead man, appeared to have been untouched.

" What do you make of the wounds ? " he asked.

" I lack your extensive experience in these matters, but I will give you my opinion, for what it is worth." I bent to examine the grisly wounds that had been inflicted on the dead man. " There are more wounds than are necessary to kill him. It is almost as if he had been sacrificed in some ritual, absurd as the idea may sound. I would have to say that from the angle, or rather from the angles, of the wounds, that more than one person was involved."

" And what of the weapon ? "

" It is hard to say. A knife of some kind. Obviously not the bread knife on this table, or the knife that has been used to slice the ham."

" Obviously not," he agreed. He brought out his lens, and peered through it at the corpse. " A single edged blade, designed more for cutting than stabbing. And a short blade, such as might be found on a seaman's or a fisherman's jack-knife."

" This would all seem to point to one particular group of people, would it not ? "

" Indeed it would, were it not for the fact that we were specifically told that they had arrived from the harbour where they had moored their boat. That should be an easy enough fact to establish."

" Or to disprove," said I.

Holmes did not reply to this, but seemed engrossed in an examination of the items on the table. " Now, where is that teapot ? " he asked, half to himself. " Aha ! " He turned to examine the small table at the entrance to the room, upon which stood a teapot covered by a tea cosy.

" What is this ? " He was referring to a small recess in one wall, covered by a curtain. He drew the curtain back, and dropped to his knees to examine the floor of the recess. " It is impossible to say if anyone has been standing here or not, but it would make a fine hiding place for an assassin, would it not ? "

" I agree. And with the victim's back to the recess, he would have no warning until it is too late."

" I think we require the assistance of at least one of the three fine young men standing outside the door. Would you be so kind as to invite one of them who discovered their mother to come here ? "

I left the room and enquired of the three brothers which of them it was who had discovered their mother. Not entirely to my surprise, it was the youngest, David, who told us that he had come across her first.

" Be so good as to follow me," I commanded, using a tone of voice that I had hardly used since my Army days, and which I knew from experience typically achieved the desired results. When we reached the room, Holmes was waiting for us outside the door.

" Excellent. Mr. David Griffiths, is it not ? " extending his hand, which was taken, a trifle diffidently.

" You are really the famous Mr. Sherlock Holmes ? " enquired the Welshman. Holmes said nothing, but nodded in reply. " Well, I can tell you that my brothers and I are innocent of anything to do with this matter. Our mother has told you that she discovered the body at half past five ? " Holmes nodded once again. " At half past five, my brothers and I were landing our boat, and we have many witnesses to prove it." His tone was angry, almost menacing.

" I am not accusing you or your brothers of anything," replied Holmes calmly. " However, I believe that you discovered your mother lying on the floor, having fainted after beholding this ghastly sight."

" That is so," admitted Griffiths.

" In which case, I would like you to take up the position in which you discovered your mother."

The other looked perplexed, and furrowed his brow. " You mean that I should lie on the floor in the same position that I discovered my mother ? "

" Precisely. Now, if you would be so good."

Griffiths arranged himself on the floor, his feet pointing into the room, lying on his back.

" You are positive that this is the position in which you found your mother ? " Holmes demanded of him.

" I am sure."

" But you were not alone when you discovered her ? "

" No, my brother Owen was with me."

" Very good. Watson, be so kind as to fetch brother Owen here. Mr. Griffiths, you may rise and return to your place at the front door."

As I walked towards the front door, David Griffiths caught up with me and tugged at my sleeve. " What is he trying to prove in this way ? "

" He is merely attempting to establish the facts of the case," I told him, though I had some suspicion that Holmes had already surmised the identity of the guilty party or parties involved. I ordered Owen Griffiths to the fatal chamber, preventing him from speaking with his brother.

Holmes repeated his request to assume the position in which he had discovered his mother. Without any hesitation, Owen Griffiths placed himself face down, his head towards the room. " Thank you," said Holmes, making yet another note in his book.

As the brother stood up, there was a noise at the door, and shortly afterwards a uniformed constable joined us.

Obviously intimidated by Holmes' air and presence, he nonetheless stood his ground and proceeded to do what he saw as his duty. " I've been told who you are, sir, and I have heard of you, but I should let you know that it is more than my job's worth to let you and this gentleman here," jerking his head at me, " into this room."

" Quite right, Sergeant," said Holmes in a conciliatory tone. " You have your duty to do, and I will step out of your way."

The constable, who had obviously been prepared for some resistance, appeared to back down a little. " I'm only a constable, begging your pardon sir. I'm sure that the inspector, when he arrives from Aberystwyth, will be happy to hear your opinions on the matter. Excuse me, sir," turning to me, " but I believe you are a doctor ? "

" I am indeed."

" Unofficially, Sir, if you wouldn't mind, have you any idea when this man died ? "

" The heat of the room has prevented me from drawing any definite conclusions on the matter, and I can only say that it is within the last two hours."

" Very good, sir. I hope that you will understand that we will require a statement from you and Mr. Holmes here in the near future ? May I also ask if you or Mr. Holmes have touched anything in this room ? "

Holmes answered for us both. " I confess that we picked

up the dead man's hand to attempt to ascertain the degree of rigor mortis. Other than that, we have touched nothing. All is as we found it."

" Thank you, sir. Now if you two gentlemen wouldn't mind ? "

We took the hint, and walked towards the door, the grandfather clock striking the half-hour as we passed it. Holmes pulled out his watch, comparing the time it displayed with that of the clock.

As we walked past the two brothers on watch outside the front door, David Griffiths grabbed my sleeve once again. " Does he know who did it ? " he asked me in a hoarse whisper which must have been audible to Holmes.

" If he does, he has not yet informed me of the fact." I disengaged myself from his grasp, and followed Holmes to our lodging.

Our landlady, Mrs. Williams, told us that Mrs. Griffiths had gone to the house of her sister, at the other end of the village, but had left word that she was willing to answer any questions that Holmes or I might see fit to put to her.

" I don't suppose you two gentlemen will require any tea after what you have just seen ? " she concluded.

" On the contrary," Holmes told her. " I am sorry to say that I have seen enough of death by violence that it fails to upset me. And Watson here has served with the Army in India, and from what he says, he is even more accustomed to such sights than am I."

" Very good. You two gentlemen must have stomachs made of cast iron. From what she was telling me just now, it was enough to make anyone sick." She bustled out of the room, remarking that she would make a fresh pot of tea.

" It worries me that the two Griffiths boys adopted such

contrary positions to indicate the attitude of their mother when she was discovered," I said to Holmes.

" What does that suggest to you ? "

" That only one of them actually discovered her. The other did not."

" What if neither of them discovered her ? " Holmes asked me. Before I could fully consider his meaning and give him an answer, he had placed the warning finger to his lips. Mrs. Williams entered, bearing the teapot.

" Well, I hope you have some kind of appetite. I'm sure that I couldn't manage to eat a thing, after all that I've heard." She placed the teapot on the table with a little more force than was strictly necessary, and left the room.

Holmes chuckled. " It seems that she suspects us of being a pair of ghouls or worse. But to return to the original subject of our discussion. What if neither of the brothers actually discovered their mother lying on the floor ? "

" Then who did discover her ? "

" Let us assume that she was never lying on the floor at all." He paused, sunk in thought for the space of about a minute. Suddenly he sprang up. " Come, Watson ! We have work to do."

" But the tea ! " I objected. " What will Mrs. Williams think of us ? "

" Blast the tea, and blast Mrs. Williams," he retorted. " She has already cast us in the worst possible light. I am sure that we can sink no lower in her estimation than we have done so at present. Come ! "

He seized his hat and stick, and strode out of the door with me in his wake, ignoring the frantic protests of our landlady. " To the harbour," he told me. It was a walk of about five minutes to the harbour, and once there we made for the small shack that served as the office of the harbourmaster. Holmes rapped on the door with his stick, and a surly elderly Welshman answered.

" What can I be doing for you at this time ? " he asked.

" My name is Sherlock Holmes," my friend informed him. " You may have heard of me."

" Oh yes. The London police agent."

Holmes was obviously irritated by this description of himself, but except to me, who knew him well, this was not apparent in his next words. " It is true that I sometimes work with the police, but I am not employed by them. However, in this particular instance, it is almost certain that the police will be asking some questions very similar to the ones I wish to ask you now."

" Such as ? " said the other, suspiciously.

" Which boat is the one operated by the Griffiths brothers ? "

For answer, the harbourmaster pointed to a white fishing smack close by. " Why do you want to know that ? "

Holmes declined to answer the question, but followed up with one of his own. " When did it return this evening ? "

" I would say about the same time as usual."

" And that would be ? " Holmes was obviously, to my eye, having difficulty keeping his temper.

" A little before six o'clock. Maybe ten minutes before. They hadn't caught any fish, I noticed that, so they just tied up the boat and started to walk home."

" Thank you," Holmes told him. " You have been most helpful."

" Aren't you going to ask me any more questions ? "

" Maybe later, but not at present," smiled my friend.

We walked away from the harbour, and were turning into the road containing the house where we were lodging, when I directed Holmes' attention to the figure in the road ahead of us. " It is the Griffiths daughter, Gwen ! "

" We must hurry," was his response, quickening his pace to overtake the young girl.

When we caught up with her, it was obvious to my eye that she was in some kind of shocked state. Her face was pale, and her breathing was irregular.

" What do you two gentlemen want ? " she demanded of us defiantly. " I had nothing to do with it, I tell you."

" My dear young lady," said Holmes smoothly. " No one is accusing you of anything. Please put your mind at rest, and answer two simple questions for me, if you would."

" I'm not going to say anything that'll put anyone else in trouble. If you want to know where I've just come from, I've been with Dai Edwards, and he and his mother and father will tell you the same."

" I wouldn't doubt you for the world," Holmes told her. " Thank you for answering one of my questions," he smiled.

" What was the other one, then ? "

" I was just going to ask you what time you left your house to visit Mr. Edwards."

At this, the girl looked sulky. " Don't know exactly. I don't have a watch, you know."

" No matter. May I give you a warning ? "

She looked at him through narrowed eyes. " What ? "

" When you go back to your house, you will find that a very unpleasant event has occurred. I would advise you not to go straight back home, but to visit Mrs. Williams at her house, or preferably, your mother is with her sister, I have been told. You may prefer to visit her there. But I would strongly advise that you do not go straight to your house."

" You know something that you are not telling me, don't you ? "

Rather than replying directly, Holmes simply repeated his advice that the girl should make her way to her aunt's house, rather than her own. She thanked him for this, though her puzzlement was obvious, and turned to go in the direction from which she had first come.

" And what do you make of that ? " I asked Holmes.

" I'm certain that she was with her sweetheart," Holmes replied. " I think it would be instructive for us to pay a visit there."

We made enquiries as to the whereabouts of the house of Mr. Dai Edwards, and a walk of a few minutes found us outside his door. However, an older man, whom we took to be the father of the sweetheart of the young girl, steadfastly refused to answer our questions. Indeed, we had no way of knowing whether he understood us at all, given that he showed no signs of comprehension, and responded to our queries only in Welsh.

" Highly frustrating," I grumbled to Holmes as we trudged our way back to the main street of the village.

Holmes started to reply, but suddenly held up his hand and we stopped. The noise of footsteps behind us grew louder, and a young man, of Herculean build, came running to meet us.

" Excuse me, gentlemen, but I heard that you were talking to my father. I am sorry, but he hardly understands any English at all, and he is not well disposed towards strangers. Maybe I can be of assistance ? "

" Thank you very much for your offer," Holmes said. " I believe you are engaged to be married to Miss Gwen Griffiths ? "

The young man twisted his hands in some

embarrassment, and his handsome face flushed red. " I would not exactly say that we were engaged to be married, but there is an understanding between us, you might say."

" It is nothing to be ashamed of," Holmes reassured him. " We were talking to Miss Williams a little while ago, and she told us that she had visited you at your house."

" That is correct."

" May I ask at what time she arrived at your house ? "

The other's face flushed an even deeper red, which I had not believed to be possible. " I cannot answer that question," he mumbled.

" Cannot, or will not ? " asked my friend, but despite his words, there was no malice in the tone.

" I cannot," Edwards stated in a firmer tone. " I gave my word to Gwen that I would not say that to anyone, unless I was under oath in court."

" Your loyalty does you proud," said Holmes. " I will not press the matter further. Thank you for your candour in this."

So saying, we shook hands with young Edwards, who returned in the direction of his house, and we resumed our path to our lodging.

" If the young lady required him to make that promise, including the exception that if he was under oath in court, then we must believe that something is being concealed."

" And what would you believe that something to be ? " Holmes asked me in return.

" Despite the fact that the Griffiths brothers seem unable to account for the disposition of their mother when they discovered her, the evidence of the harbourmaster and all the other fishermen who saw their boat return must make them innocent. Having seen young Edwards, and listened to his story, can we believe that it is any other than he ?

Consider, Fuller was probably paying his unwelcome attentions to Miss Griffiths. Edwards calls at the house, maybe by appointment, or maybe the visit was unannounced.
In any case he witnesses what he sees as an unforgivable
act committed against his beloved. He knows the house,
having been a constant visitor. He knows a place where he
can remain concealed, and he waits till his victim is seated
and unsuspecting before he falls on him with a jack-knife
and in a fit of passion repeatedly stabs him, before making his escape, taking Miss Griffiths with him. Mrs. Griffiths brings in the tea, sees the gory scene before her, and
falls in a faint until she is revived by her returning sons,
who not unnaturally are confused about the details of the
discovery."

" Well, well, Watson. I must applaud you on your appli-
cation of logic to the facts that you have observed."

" Then I am correct ? "

" No, you are completely in error. You have failed to observe several very significant facts, the presence of which
serves to completely overturn your idea. But," observing
my crestfallen face, " you have come to your conclusion,
incomplete though it may be, in a most workmanlike and
competent manner at a speed which greatly exceeds that
of the average police blockhead. Had you only taken the
trouble to look a little more carefully at certain objects in
the room, no doubt you would have reached the correct
conclusion."

" In other words, the conclusion you have reached ? "
I asked, more than a little bitterly. Sherlock Holmes,
though he was not always aware of the fact, was sometimes
more than a little cutting in his criticism of others.

On this occasion, however, my tone of voice registered
with him. " I apologise, Watson. Your analysis is indeed

excellent as far as it goes. The fact that it did not go far enough is more a matter of my habits than any deficiency of yours. Fear not, all will be explained soon enough." He clapped me on the shoulder in a friendly fashion, and it was hard for me to maintain my resentment, given his conciliatory attitude.

On our arrival at our lodgings, we discovered a small portly man in an ill fitting bowler hat waiting in the drawing room. He introduced himself as Inspector Evans, and greeted Sherlock Holmes coldly enough.

" I think that we have solved this case, thank you very much, Mr. Holmes," were almost his first words to us. " It's the girl's sweetheart, Dai Edwards. Jealousy at her flirting with the sophisticated visitor. We'll have him arrested and in court within the hour."

" How very interesting that you should think that way," Holmes said to him. " Dr. Watson here was saying much the same thing."

" How gratifying to have London confirming my deductions," said the policeman.

" This part of London finds your deductions to be completely in error," Holmes answered him. " If you arrest young Edwards, you will be a laughing stock all the way from Harlech to Cardiff." These words seemed to take the inspector aback.

" Then whom do you suspect ? " he asked, obviously less sure of himself than he had been previously.

" I suspect no one," Holmes answered equably, putting a slight emphasis on the word " suspect". " I am positive that I know the identity of the murderers."

" If you are thinking the Griffiths lads are guilty of the crime, then I have to tell you that you are mistaken.

They were out at sea in their boat when the murder was committed."

" On the contrary. They were in the room when the murder was committed, because they were the ones committing the murder," asserted Holmes. " I take it you have examined the scene of the murder ? "

" Of course."

" You observed the spots of blood on the tablecloth ? "

" I did indeed."

" Did you also observe that some of those spots lay under the rim of the plate, in such a location that they could not have been made when the plate was in that position ? I remember one of the bloodstains being half under the plate. There is no way that that could have occurred unless the plate had been placed over the bloodstain after it had been made."

" Perhaps I was a little hasty in my examination," said the Inspector, and his voice now sounded very unsure."

" Never mind," Holmes reassured him. " No doubt you have interviewed Mrs. Griffiths ? " The other nodded. " How do you understand that the body was discovered ? "

" She left the deceased sitting at the table, and left the room to fetch something, and when she returned, the deceased was—"

" —deceased ? " offered Holmes, not without a certain malice, which the inspector chose to ignore.

" Whereupon, she fainted and remained unconscious until revived by her sons, who had just returned from their fishing."

" Do you remember what it was that she was carrying when she entered the room ? "

" Yes, it was the teapot."

" Ah yes, the teapot," remarked Holmes. " Watson, I

realise that this may prove an impossible piece of thespian virtuosity, but I wish you to put yourself in the place of Mrs. Griffiths. You have left a gentleman sitting in front of his tea. You have returned, holding a fresh pot of tea, of some considerable weight. You did observe the size and the quality of the teapot, did you not ? Good. You open the door, and you see for yourself that your guest is sitting at the table, dripping gore, obviously slain by an unknown assailant. What do you do ? "

I closed my eyes, and considered the matter. " Having seen the woman in question, I would probably sink to the floor in a hysterical fit."

Holmes clapped his hands together. " Absolutely. Your thoughts and mine run in parallel on this matter. You would not, for example, consider placing the teapot on a small table, having first ensured that there was a mat placed underneath to protect the polish of the table, before sinking senseless to the floor ? "

" Indeed I would not."

" And yet, such was the case."

The inspector looked puzzled. " You are telling me that she had the presence of mind to seek out a mat and place it on a table before placing the teapot on it and then collapsing to the floor ? "

" Not at all, my dear Inspector. I am telling you that she never collapsed to the floor at all. The whole story of her faint is a complete fabrication. Let me tell you of something else." Holmes then proceeded to relate to the inspector the story of how the two Griffiths sons had given contradictory accounts of how they had discovered their mother at the entrance to the room.

" Well," said the policeman, after much thought and

scratching of his head. " This certainly does put a differ-ent complexion on things, does it not ? "

" Indeed it does. Most notably, it casts considerable doubt on the timing of the death."

" Well, since you seem to have demolished my theory and that of Dr. Watson here, perhaps you would be good enough to let us know what you believe happened."

" With pleasure," Holmes said to him, leaning back in his chair in that easy attitude that I knew so well. Outside the window, I could hear a wind starting to rise, and the first patter of drops of rain falling. " What I believe hap-pened, and I am confident that events will bear me out, is that Fuller had been paying his unwelcome attentions to Miss Gwen Griffiths. She had complained about this to her brothers, who were determined to take their revenge on him. They enlisted the help of her mother to set the scene, and to divert the attention of any investigator, other than an alert member of the species, such as yourself, Inspec-tor," he smiled. " The plan was that their mother would announce that Fuller's evening meal would be served at about the time she and her sons had arranged for the fish-ermen to return home. Her task was to seat the guest in the dining room, where he would wait, unsuspecting, for his meal. I have a feeling that Miss Gwen Griffiths was also involved here, maybe as an inducement to keep him in the room."

" That would explain why young Edwards had been sworn to secrecy regarding the time at which she visited him," I broke in.

" Precisely so. If she was an accomplice, she would need an alibi, and young Edwards strikes me as being a perfectly straightforward and honest young man whose affection for his young lady would guarantee her safety."

" And the whole business of setting the table with the food was an elaborate ruse to deceive us all regarding the time of death, and to provide an alibi for the three Williams lads ? " said the police officer.

" You have summed up the matter most admirably, Inspector. Mrs. Griffiths never fell to the floor in any faint, but being good housekeeper that she is, the idea of dropping a teapot full of tea onto her carpet was too much for her." He rose, and closed the window. " Dear me, I believe we are going to have quite a storm. Is it not strange how the human mind works ? Here is a woman who had quite coldly and calculatedly planned the death of a man, but found it impossible to allow a teapot to fall to the floor." He shrugged. " Such are the peculiarities of human nature." His last words were punctuated by a flash of lightning, followed a few seconds afterwards by a roll of thunder. " By George ! That sounded close."

" I have to admit, Mr. Holmes, that everything you have said makes perfect sense to me. When I looked at the body, it was difficult to see that one person could have committed all those atrocities, but if the work were divided between three, it makes much more sense. May I count on you and Dr. Watson to assist myself and Constable Evans with the arrests ? "

" I would prefer to remain in the background unless my assistance is absolutely required," I objected. " I spent some time in the company of David Griffiths, and even if he is guilty of the crime as we suspect, I would be reluctant to take part in his arrest."

Rather to my surprise, Holmes seemed to agree with me. " I concur with Watson here. Naturally, I will do my duty as a citizen if asked, but unless you feel that my presence is absolutely necessary, I would likewise prefer not to become involved."

" I do not think that Constable Evans will find this an easy task either," commented the Inspector. " He is from this village, and has grown up with the lads he has to arrest."

" He knew that such a thing was a possibility when he joined the Force," remarked Holmes coldly. " Watson and I are still free men in that regard."

" Very good. I will whistle for you if you are needed." So saying, the inspector strode out of the room, calling for the constable as he went. His departure was marked by another lightning flash and crash of thunder. By now, the wind and rain had both increased in intensity.

Another flash of lightning and crack of thunder, and the inspector reappeared. " They've gone ! " he exclaimed. " It seems that they have gone down to the harbour."

" Surely they would never put to sea in this storm," I objected. " They would never escape."

" They might escape justice," Holmes pointed out.

" You mean... ? "

" I mean simply that they may put to sea with no intention of ever returning."

S IT TURNED OUT, this is what eventually transpired. The three Griffiths brothers had indeed taken out their fishing boat into the worsening storm. Despite the entreaties of the police, no volunteer could be found to follow them out to sea, and neither they nor their boat were ever seen again.

The little Welsh inspector, whose attitude towards

Holmes had completely changed, took note of Holmes' recommendation that no prosecution be mounted against Mrs. Griffiths or her daughter, chiefly on the grounds that any evidence against them would be chiefly circumstantial.

We left the village of Abernetty two days after the events described above, much to the relief, I believe, of Mrs. Williams, who regarded us as birds of ill omen.

On the train returning to London, I could not help remarking to Holmes that I had been impressed by the speed with which he had come to the correct conclusion. " How," I asked him, " did you first come to the realisation that the table had been laid following the death of Fuller, and not before ? Was it the bloodstains ? "

Sherlock Holmes laughed. " It was not that. It was something so trivial and so ludicrous that I restrained from mentioning it to the Inspector. You remember that that afternoon and evening were excessively warm ? Indeed in that house it was even warmer. Do you remember the custom of our landlady in decorating the butter which was provided for us to spread on our bread ? "

" Indeed I do. There was a charming little sprig of parsley on top of the pats of butter."

" Indeed. I do not know if it is a custom of the locality, or whether the Williams household had copied the habit of the Griffiths family, or whether it was the other way round, but at any rate, Mrs. Griffiths likewise adorned her butter with a touch of greenery. Had that plate of butter sat on the table for the length of time that we had been told, the parsley would have sunk into the butter to a considerable extent. As it was, it was relatively untouched. This suggested to me that the butter had been placed on the table comparatively recently. And if the butter, I reasoned, why not the whole of the meal ? From there, everything fell into place." He leaned back in his seat and drew contentedly on his pipe. " Ah, how good it will be to return to the peace and quiet of London after the hurly-burly of the Welsh countryside."

Sherlock Holmes
and the Case of the
Finsbury House

EDITOR'S NOTE

This story was bound in manuscript form in a sealed envelope. It describes the adventure referred to in The Norwood Builder *as " the shocking affair of the Dutch steamship* Friesland, *which so nearly cost us both our lives". Shocking it certainly is, and not simply for the crimes described in it. What was particularly shocking to me when I read this account was Holmes' cavalier regard for Watson's safety. Though he offers an apology to his friend, Watson does not record or even indicate that he fully accepts it, and it is possible that the incident rankled somewhat, possibly sufficiently for it to be excluded from the tales that Watson released to the public.*

There was no title attached to this adventure, so I have taken the liberty of entitling it The Finsbury House.

Y FRIEND, the famous consulting detective Sherlock Holmes, had often displayed to me his interest in and knowledge of the musical world. I was, however, unaware of his interest in the more visual arts until the events related here, which formed the prologue to one of the more sensational and dangerous adventures in which he and I found ourselves involved.

I had recently been away from London, taking the air at a seaside resort. Holmes claimed to be immersed in a case of extraordinary delicacy, and did not accompany me. On my return following a week away from the metropolis, I entered our rooms at Baker-street to discover Holmes stretched at full length on the floor, face-down, examining what appeared to be a large painting through one of his lenses.

He greeted me with an absorbed air, without, however, bothering to turn his head or even to glance in my direction. " Welcome back, Watson. Home is the sailor, home from the sea. I trust that your little holiday romance ended satisfactorily ? "

Though it was true that I had made the acquaintance of a charming young lady during my time at Broadstairs, I had not mentioned this to Holmes in my communications to him, and my astonishment must have registered in my face.

" The flower in your buttonhole, Watson. I have noticed that when a young man's fancy, or even when your fancy, strays in the direction of romance, unaccustomed foliage tends to sprout in that area. There is also a decided spring in your step which cannot be wholly attributable to the effects of the sea air."

" You have hardly taken the trouble to glance in my direction since I entered the room," I pointed out.

" The trivial details that I have just remarked are perfectly clear to me, even when reflected in the surface of this lens, which constitutes an excellent mirror," he retorted.

" Leaving the question of my affections entirely to one side, may I enquire what on earth you are doing ? I confess that I had no idea that you are interested in matters such as this."

" All is grist to my mill where a case is involved. I have found myself in this position of being an expert in the arts owing to the force of circumstances, rather than as a result of choice on my part, though I confess that the subject of forgery in art presents its own particular interests, which could well repay further study at some time in the future. What do you make of this ? " He asked me, springing to his feet and taking the picture, leaning it against the back of the sofa for my inspection.

" I do not pretend to be any kind of expert in these things," I told him. I regarded the picture, which was a portrait of a man in Stuart costume, somewhat in the Dutch style. " If I was asked to give any kind of opinion, though, I would say that this was a 17th-century work, possibly the work of van Dyck, or one of his contemporaries."

" Bravo, Watson ! Bravo indeed. This portrait is indeed attributed to van Dyck. However, it is my considered opinion that it has been painted in the last few years—possibly even in the last year."

" And the owner of the painting wishes to verify its authenticity ? " I asked. " Surely it would be better for him to employ an expert in these matters ? Meaning no offence to you, my dear Holmes, but you are hardly widely regarded as being an authority on matters of art."

" By no means. This is a matter which has come to my attention almost by accident, as the result of my investigations into a case which would appear to have no connection at all with the world of art. Until two days ago, this painting was hanging in the gallery of Amberfield House."

" The London home of Sir Godfrey Leighbury ? "

" The same. Sir Godfrey had employed my services in a most delicate matter. His wife, Lady Celia, appeared to have mislaid a valuable diamond brooch, but was unable to tell him, or so it would appear, where the loss had occurred. On my examining the case, it was obvious to me that she was perfectly able to inform him of the whereabouts of the brooch, but was unwilling to do so. After a little time I was able to locate the brooch—she had inadvertently given me some clues as to its whereabouts—but it proved to have been set with false stones."

" I take it that originally it had been created using real diamonds ? "

" So I was informed, though, of course, I have no way of confirming this, other than the facts that the jewellery was insured, and that presumably the insurance company had made an accurate estimate of the brooch's value. I informed Sir Godfrey of my findings, though it is not usually my place to come between husband and wife in such matters.

" I took the opportunity of investigating further, and my suspicions were aroused when I observed that at least one of the paintings in the gallery had recently been removed and replaced. I enquired of Sir Godfrey whether any of the paintings had been taken down for restoration or for any other reason, but he was unable to confirm this. With his permission, therefore, I removed the painting which had originally attracted my attention, and arranged for it to be sent here where I could examine it at leisure. From what I can see, it appears that my suspicions were well founded."

" You believe it to be a forgery, then ? "

" I am almost certain of it. Oil paintings of a certain age exhibit cracks in their surface, the technical term for which is *craquelure*. Within those cracks, it is natural for dust to accumulate over the years. Although this painting exhibits cracks resembling the type of pattern I would expect to see on a work of art of this age, there is little or no dust within the cracks. This leads me to believe that the painting is a recent one. Will you accompany me to the National Gallery, where I wish to make a similar examination of a painting which is authentically the work of van Dyck ? "

" By all means. Do you wish to leave now ? "

" No, no. I wish you to observe for yourself the phenomenon about which I speak. There are also one or two other small matters to which I must attend. Here," passing me the lens, " although it is somewhat easier to see the dust when the painting is lying flat, as it was when you entered the room, you should still be able to make out the fact that there is little of the accumulated debris that one might expect in a painting over two centuries old."

I looked, but to tell the truth I was somewhat unsure what Holmes expected me to observe. It did appear to me, though, that the painting was remarkably free of dirt and grime when it was scrutinised through Holmes' high-powered lens. " And the painting has not been cleaned or restored ? " I asked him.

" Certainly not in Sir Godfrey's lifetime. It is obvious to me that the original painting has been substituted, and this forgery has taken its place. It is possible that this is the only painting in the gallery where this has occurred, but I fear, from my earlier observations, that there are at least two more works of art where this substitution has been carried out. But before I can pronounce definitively on the matter, it will be necessary for us to make a comparison with the painting of similar age. Hence my proposed visit to the National Gallery."

" If I understand correctly, you believe that the valuable *objets d'art* and trinkets belonging to Sir Godfrey's family have been disposed of, and their loss disguised by their replacement with these counterfeits ? "

" Precisely."

" But to what end ? "

" That, Watson, is a matter of extreme delicacy, and I am unwilling in many ways to dip my toe into these waters. Lady Celia, as I am sure you are well aware from your perusal of the Society pages, is a favourite at Court, and if this is a matter of blackmail, however discreet I may be in my enquiries, it is inevitable that some attention will be drawn to the matter. At this time when the political situation is so delicate with regard to so many matters, such attention would be a welcome weapon in the hands of the Radicals, a weapon with which I am not prepared to furnish them."

With that, he fell silent, and I busied myself with unpacking my luggage. I had almost finished this task when I looked up to see Holmes standing by my bed-room door, inviting me to join him on the visit to the Gallery.

Once we had arrived, Holmes' conduct was singular enough to attract the attention of other visitors, though on our arrival he had previously explained his proposed course of action to the curators. Bringing his lens close to the surface of several paintings contemporary with the supposed van Dyck, he examined them closely. " Were I permitted to do so, I would take samples of the dirt that has accumulated here," he told me, " but it will become plain to you, should you examine these paintings closely, that the supposed van Dyck in our rooms at Baker-street is a modern copy." He passed the glass to me, and I bent to the surface of the painting, enjoying, I must admit, the scandalised gasps of some of the other visitors behind me. I overheard one of them whisper to another that Holmes and I must be anarchists, bent on some dastardly plot, and I smiled to myself as I concentrated on the work of art in front of me. Indeed, as Holmes had said, the cracks in the painting's surface were filled with the dust of ages, and the cracks themselves appeared to be of a somewhat different pattern to those I had seen in the picture at Baker-street. Handing the lens back to Holmes, I remarked on this fact, and he smiled.

" Good. I think there is now no doubt in either of our

minds. Thank you, ladies, gentlemen," he said to the gaping crowd which had now assembled behind us, turning to address them directly. " The performance has ended, and we are now returning to the place whence we came." With a sardonic smile on his face, he swept through the mass of visitors, leaving me to follow in his wake.

" And now where ? " I asked, as we existed the building into Trafalgar-square.

" I think Sir Godfrey should be informed of our conclusions. I am guessing he will be at his club, the Army and Navy. A stroll to Pall-mall ? "

The weather being fine, I assented to this suggestion, and in a few minutes we were entering the portals of the famous establishment, and enquiring of the porter whether Sir Godfrey Leighbury was on the premises. A page was dispatched in search of him, bearing Holmes' card, and soon returned with the news that Sir Godfrey would be delighted to see us.

Sir Godfrey, whom I was meeting for the first time, was a tall, thin, pale-faced man, clean-shaven, and carrying himself with a military bearing. Considering his looks and his thinning hair, I put his age at about fifty, considerably older than his wife, who was invariably described as being " young" and " beautiful"; adjectives which could not be said to describe her husband with any degree of accuracy.

" I would prefer it, Sir Godfrey, if we could speak in private," said Holmes. " What I have to tell you may be a little upsetting to you, and it is quite likely that you will not wish others to hear."

" Very well, if you must," said the retired officer, leading us to one of the private rooms opening off the smoking-room. " A drink for you fellows ? No ? Very good, then. Proceed, Holmes."

" I fear to tell you," said Holmes gently, " that my original suspicions were correct. The painting attributed to van Dyck is a modern reproduction, and I would be very surprised if it were the only such painting in your collection."

Sir Godfrey gasped. " But that painting has been in the family for the past two hundred years ! " he objected. " Surely it cannot be any kind of forgery ? "

" It has been replaced. Recently, I would say."

" This is totally outrageous ! " The veins on Sir Godfrey's forehead stood out, and I feared that he was about to suffer some sort of seizure. " You are sure of this, Holmes ? "

" You should call independent experts in the field, Sir Godfrey, but I would stake my professional reputation that this is the case. Maybe my methods for detecting such an imposture may differ from those that they employ, but I can assure you that they bring the same results."

" And how many of the paintings have been substituted ? "

" From the brief examination I made at Amberfield House, I would say that there are several others which may be in the same condition."

The other sunk his face in his hands. " And the diamonds from the brooch ? "

" I have no news of them."

" Are you sure you will not join me in a whisky and soda ? I feel I am in need of some kind of restorative."

This time, Holmes and I accepted his invitation, and Sir Godfrey rang the bell and placed an order for our drinks. We sat in silence until the decanter and syphon had been brought to us, and Sir Godfrey played host, dispensing the refreshments.

" What do you propose doing, Holmes ? " he asked,

having taken a pull at his drink, which appeared to restore a little of the colour to his face. " Can you tell me when this substitution of the paintings would have taken place ? "

" I think we can be certain that it was at a time when you were absent for a protracted period. The time needed to make the preparatory studies for a copy and then to execute such a copy, before replacing the original in the frame with the copy, would require a considerable amount of time, in my opinion. In the past two or three years, is there any such time when you have not visited the house for, say, two months on end ? "

" Why, yes. I was appointed as an attaché to our Embassy in The Hague as a temporary appointment. Celia did not wish to live with me in the Netherlands, though she made frequent visits, and I held the position for nearly a year, returning to England some years ago. You believe the substitution was made at that time ? "

" I am certain of it."

" But who would have done such a thing ? " Holmes said nothing in answer to this query, but fixed the baronet with a steady gaze. " Celia ? But why ? " asked Sir Godfrey.

" I have come across many reasons in the course of my career why such actions are undertaken," explained Holmes. " Almost without exception, I fear that they are ones which the perpetrators of the substitutions would sooner not have noised abroad."

I watched Sir Godfrey as Holmes' meaning sank in. " Blackmail ? " gasped the other. His face had now turned to an alarming brick-red colour, and he was breathing hard through his nose. " By God, if I find the blackguard who is doing this, his life will not be worth living ! I will make the scoundrel wish he had never been born."

" Gently, gently," Holmes calmed him. " Your sentiments do you credit, but I can assure you from my experience of these matters that this is not the way to approach
such a problem. Such rogues—and believe me, I fully
share your opinion of the despicable specimens who practice such felonies—will immediately strike back with the
information they hold, should they feel themselves threatened. Seeking revenge in this manner would be like putting your hand into a nest of vipers, my dear sir. With all
due respect, I strongly advise allowing me to handle the
business for you ? "

" You and not the official police ? "

" With all due respect to the officers of the official police
force, though they do not lack bravery and tenacity, they
are sadly deficient in reasoning power, and in the intelligent extraction of facts from evidence. Maybe there will be
a need to involve the police when all has been revealed, and
matters are safely under control."

" I see," said Sir Godfrey. " And no doubt you wish me
to foot the bill for these investigations of yours ? " His
tone was somewhat accusatory.

" By no means, Sir Godfrey," replied Holmes light-
ly. " When I bring the case to a satisfactory conclusion,"
(there was a snort from the other at this, which seemed to
indicate derision) " you may feel inclined to increase my
fee from what we have already agreed, but it already appears to me that this is one of those cases where the solution will largely constitute its own reward."

" I believe that understand you," repeated the other.
" What do you wish me to do ? "

" At present, I merely require your permission to visit your house and question your servants. However, to
avoid arousing suspicion, I will not be conducting such

interviews in my own person. If you should chance to come across any of your servants in converse with a somewhat seedy-looking groom or some such, please have the kindness not to interrupt the conversation. It is more than likely that it will be I to whom they are talking."

" And my wife, Celia ? I do not believe that you will adopt such a disguise in order to interview her."

" Currently, I have no plans to talk to her, in my own character or in any other. However, should it appear to me that it is necessary to talk to her, I shall ask your permission in advance of doing so."

" Very good. I can see, Holmes, that you have the manners of a gentleman, though your trade, if I may speak frankly, is not to my mind one which it is entirely proper for a gentleman to pursue."

" Be that as it may," my friend replied brusquely, " as I said earlier, I would strongly recommend that you bring in additional experts in artistic matters to examine your paintings, some of which, as I mentioned, are probably copies, rather than the originals. If I may add a further recommendation, I would suggest that this be done while Lady Celia is absent, and that the knowledge of this is kept from her. By the by, the van Dyck currently reposing in my rooms will be returned to you in the next day or so."

" I thank you for your advice on this matter. I will certainly be taking it, since you appear to know what you are doing here."

" As matters further unfold themselves, I shall be making regular reports, addressed to you here at this club. I feel it would be unwise, if not somewhat premature, if Lady Celia were to learn of my involvement at this stage. There will be time enough for that anon. Come, Watson," he added, swallowing the last of his drink, " we must be on our way. My thanks for your hospitality, sir. I hope to have good news for you soon."

OR THE NEXT WEEK, I saw little of Sherlock Holmes. He left Baker-street early, dressed as a common workman, and returned late. I guessed that he was executing the plan he had outlined earlier of interrogating the servants at Amberfield House without their being aware that the famous Sherlock Holmes was questioning them.

He confirmed this on the evening of the fourth day of these activities.

" It has been an exceedingly tiresome day," he complained to me as he sat in his favourite armchair, clad in more respectable attire. " For the whole morning, I was informed at excruciating length of the progress of Mrs. Wigmore's lumbago—Mrs. Wigmore being the cook at Amberfield House, you understand. Even you Watson, in your capacity as a doctor, would have found the subject to be of a nature beyond description as regards its stultifying powers. And in the afternoon I have been forced to rebuff, in as gentle a fashion as possible without causing offence, the attentions of one of the housemaids, who has a pleasant enough face to look on, to be sure, but is without a brain in her head. For some reason she has decided that I am the man with whom she wishes to spend the rest of her life. The feeling, I assure you, is far from being reciprocated." He drew on his pipe, and exhaled a great cloud of blue smoke. " But we progress, Watson, we progress."

" You have learned something, then ? "

" Other than details regarding the symptoms of

lumbago ? " he laughed. " Indeed. It would appear that Lady Celia has taken herself out of the house on many occasions when her husband is away from London, or out of the country. These absences occurred at night, typically from about nine o'clock until the small hours of the morning."

" Where did she go ? "

" That is a question to which none of the servants could supply an answer. She prepared herself as if for a ball, they say, and waited for a four-wheeler to draw up outside the door, whereupon she slipped outside, and entered the vehicle, which then drove off. She returned at about four or five in the morning by the same method."

" And none of the servants has any idea of the identity of the owner of the carriage or of its destination ? "

" That is correct. These nocturnal visits seem to have been sporadic in nature. Lady Celia would go out every night for three or maybe four nights on end, and then the pattern would cease for a week or more. On those other nights, she either took her own carriage, or remained at home. On no occasion, mark you, did she leave the house in this way while Sir Godfrey was in residence."

" This has all the markings of a vulgar intrigue, does it not ? "

" Some of them, it is true. But it does not explain the way in which all activity ceases for a while before resuming. In any event, I noted a few dates. May I prevail on you to visit the newspaper offices and look through the Society reports for those dates and those surrounding them. I wish to ascertain which social gatherings, if any, Lady Celia has attended at these times."

" Have you made any progress with regard to the substituted paintings ? "

" Indeed I have. A Mr. Visser—a Dutch name, by the way—was admitted on a number of occasions in Sir Godfrey's absence. I have spoken with the footman responsible, and from the description I obtained, it appears that this Dutchman was carrying some sort of artist's equipment with him when he made his visits. Not only that, but he appeared some two months later with a couple of workmen, carrying a large square package. This last was repeated on a number of occasions before Sir Godfrey's return."

" The implication being that this Visser was responsible for producing the copies of the paintings which have been substituted for the originals ? "

" Precisely. Mynheer Visser, if that is his real name, should be the next object of my investigation, I feel. But first, if you would, Watson, I would very much appreciate any answers you can retrieve from the newspapers, while I continue my researches among the denizens of Amberfield House."

I spent an exhausting morning in the newspaper offices carrying out Holmes' request. It appeared to me that Lady Celia was missing from the lists of guests at functions on many, but not all, of the dates when the mysterious carriage had spirited her away. On the other hand, her name did appear in the lists for functions held on some of the other dates, when she had, according to Holmes' researches, taken her own carriage for the evening's entertainment.

" It seems to me, Holmes," I reported to him that evening, " that Lady Celia's entertainment is quite probably what you suspected—a series of assignations which would certainly constitute grounds for blackmail."

" There is one problem with that idea, though," was his rejoinder. " It is the episodic nature, if we may term it so, of the assignations. Can we believe that the lady's ardour, or that of her supposed lover, wanes and waxes in such a fashion ? There appears to be little rhyme or reason here. I am not such an expert in affairs of the heart as are you, Watson," and here he gave me a slight wink of the eye, indicating that he was indulging in a little gentle " chaff" at my expense, " but it would seem to me that this is a very strange way of carrying on a love affair."

" Indeed it is," I agreed, " and I can think of no reason for it."

" While I suggest that we retain the idea of a love affair as a possibility in our minds, I recommend that we also examine other options as they come to us."

" But with no definite lead to follow, other than this Mynheer Visser, the task seems hopeless," I exclaimed.

" Not so, Watson. We must set a trap. I will propose to Sir Godfrey that he remove himself from the vicinity of London, thereby opening the way for Lady Celia to follow these inclinations of hers."

" If it is indeed a love affair," I pointed out, " it may have cooled by now, and we will see no results."

Holmes shrugged. " This is possible, of course, and we must not discount the likelihood of such a state of affairs. However, it is possible that a love affair is not the explanation of the problem. At any event, we will lose nothing by carrying out this stratagem. Once Sir Godfrey is safely away, the mouse, I trust, will start to play, and you and I will keep watch over her antics. I feel there is little more of value to be gained by my continuing my visits to the servants' hall at Amberfield House. It will disappoint my pretty-faced little housemaid, I am sure, but for myself, I will feel much relieved to be out of her sights."

Holmes put these words into practice, sending a telegram

to Sir Godfrey inviting him to visit Baker-street, where he explained what he had discovered so far, and invited the other to remove himself to his country seat in Norfolk.

The baronet seemed to be unsurprised by Holmes' report and his suggestion. " As it happens, I was thinking of doing exactly that. The pheasant season starts soon, and I want to be well-prepared for it. You say it is unlikely that Celia is conducting an affair, you say ? Not that I would be surprised if she was doing so, mark you. I suppose you could describe our marital status as a ' December and May' kind of business, and I am sure I fail to provide her with the kind of amusing company that she no doubt expects."

" I did not say that it was altogether out of the question," replied Holmes, " but I am emphasising the point that it is not the only possibility in this instance. In any case, I will send full reports to you in Norfolk as new facts come to light."

" I appreciate any attempt to spare my feelings, but I can assure you that at my time of life there is no necessity for you to do so. In any case, if my leaving this pestilential hole of London will assist your investigations, I am more than happy to help you in this way."

" Sir Godfrey is hardly a lover of our capital," I remarked to Holmes following our visitor's departure.

" I cannot conceive of living outside London," he answered me. " I require the raw energy that emanates from this throbbing and pulsating dynamo at the heart of our Empire in order to stimulate my mental powers. The idea of a placid bucolic existence on the Sussex Downs, say, is one that utterly fails to appeal to me."

" Maybe when you are older," I laughed, " such an uneventful life may have its attractions."

" We will no doubt see in good time," he smiled. " In

any event, I feel that we will now be able to trace the path of Lady Celia's nocturnal excursions. I do not expect them to commence immediately that on Sir Godfrey's departure from the metropolis, but I do not expect you will object to a few nights' inconvenience in a good cause while we watch and wait, eh, Watson ? "

" You mean to watch Amberfield House and follow this mysterious four-wheeler to its destination when it makes an appearance ? "

" I do indeed. I trust you will keep me company ? "

" Indeed I will," I replied warmly. " If for no other reason than that my curiosity is aroused by this case."

N THE EVENT, we had four fruitless nights of waiting before our patience was rewarded. For those four nights we had concealed ourselves in the shadows of the square facing Amberfield House, watching for any entrance or exit. A hansom cab was waiting in the street around the corner, prepared to follow our quarry, but we had drawn four successive blanks, the cabman accepting the sovereigns that Holmes pressed into his hand at the end of each watch with an air of amused resignation at what he perceived as our folly.

I myself was yet to be convinced that our vigils would produce a result, but at half past nine o'clock, on the fifth night, the four-wheeler of which Holmes had been informed drew up outside Amberfield House. Holmes gripped me by the shoulder and hissed in my ear, " This is it, Watson. Inform the cabbie that we will be setting off in pursuit soon. I will join you immediately the carriage moves off with Lady Celia in it."

I slipped round the corner and informed the drowsy driver to prepare himself. In a matter of minutes, Holmes came hurrying around the corner. " Quick, cabby ! " he called up as he swung himself into the cab. Follow that four-wheeler which is just taking the Marylebone-road."

We were forced to drive at a good pace to keep up with our quarry, heading eastward along the Euston-road and the Pentonville-road, before turning into Finsbury, and driving along Green Lanes, by the side of the park there.

" This is not an area where I would expect a gathering to be held for those of Lady Celia's rank," I exclaimed.

" I agree. We are definitely moving in unexpected circles. Ha ! Stop here, cabbie," he addressed himself to our driver, alighting from the cab, which halted some hundred yards away from our quarry, which had drawn up outside a row of suburban houses. The driver of the four-wheeler jumped down to open the door for his passenger. To my surprise, four women descended, all dressed in what appeared from this distance to be fashionable costume, and entered the house at the end of the row where the road crosses the small river, outside which the carriage had stopped. Once the door of the house had closed behind the visitors, the driver remounted his seat and drove away.

" Four ? " I could not refrain from exclaiming. " Do you recognise any of them ? "

" The number came as a surprise to me also," admitted Holmes. " Lady Celia alone boarded the carriage at Amberfield House. The others were obviously already inside the carriage, and I cannot identify any of them in this light. One thing now seems certain, though."

" That being ? "

" This is no simple *affaire*. A woman conducting such a liaison does not bring her chaperones with her."

" Very true," I answered. " Then what is happening, do you think ? "

" It is impossible to tell at this point in the proceedings. We will make a note of the address of this house, and visit tomorrow, in the hope of obtaining some clues."

We rejoined our cab, which carried us back to Baker-street.

" Do you want me to come round and do the same to-morrow night ? " asked the driver.

" Thank you, no," answered Holmes, " but it is certainly possible I will require your services again."

" It'll be a pleasure, sir," the jarvey said in reply. " I ha-ven't been given so much money for doing nothing for a long time."

" Excellent. If you can give me an address where I may contact you in the future, I would be obliged," slipping the man a couple of sovereigns. " And in the meantime, if you could pass the word around and make discreet enquir-ies about the four-wheeler we saw just which we followed to Finsbury, without mentioning my name or anything about me, you may be sure that such information will be rewarded."

" Very good, sir, I will see what I can find out." He touched his hand to the brim of his cap and rattled off into the night.

" Heigh-ho," said Holmes to me, yawning. " Tomorrow will see the resolution of the mystery."

However, he was mistaken in this. In the morning we made our way to the house in Finsbury, and discovered the house to be adorned with a large notice proclaiming that the property was to let; a sign which we had not observed in the dark of the previous evening.

" This is puzzling, indeed," I remarked to Holmes. " I

am certain that this is the house which we visited last night, and yet it appears to be unoccupied."

" Curious," he agreed. " This is certainly the house at which the carriage stopped last night, and which the passengers entered. And the door was opened to them by someone who was already inside the house. Come, let us make our way to the letting-agent and make some enquiries about this place."

Upon Holmes, in the character of a prospective tenant, enquiring of Mr. Johnstone, whose name was on the board outside the house, the house-agent was happy to inform Holmes of some details regarding the property.

" It's been up for rent for the past three years now, and there's been a good number of people who've been interested in taking the place. But the problem is that the landlord, a Mr. de Vries, always seems to find some reason why he doesn't want to let to them. If truth be told, I'd be more than happy to see the property off my books, as it's more trouble than it's worth for me to keep it there."

" No-one lives there at present ? "

" Not for the past three years. That's when it came vacant, and Mr. de Vries came to us and signed the contract with us to advertise it to let. He's asking a good fair price for it, too, but he insists on meeting the prospective tenants personally, and every blessed time there's something that he doesn't like about them. This one has children, and he doesn't want children, that one works in a bank, and he doesn't like bankers. Why, one time he even turned down an offer from a man because he didn't like the shape of his hat, would you believe ? And it's not for want of offering money, either. Some of those he has turned down have offered a good deal more than the money he's asking."

" A strange sort of landlord," Holmes agreed smilingly.

" I take it you would have no objection to our looking over the property ? "

" None whatsoever. But I have to warn you gentlemen that you are not likely to persuade Mr. de Vries to let the place to you. Would you like me to show you over the place ? "

" There will be no need for that, I think. We will look the place over and return the key to you in an hour or so. Will that be satisfactory ? "

" Indeed it will. I will just prepare you an order to view, in the event of any concerned citizen observing you entering an empty house."

We walked back to the house, armed with the key and the piece of paper signed by Mr. Johnstone.

" Once again, we come across a Dutch name," Holmes mused aloud as we ascended the steps leading to the front door. " First, we have a Visser involved with the paintings, and now a de Vries. A coincidence, or a connection ? " He stopped short as we reached the door. " Observe, Watson. Traces of some substance on the step here. It appears as though this has been deposited recently." He bent and scraped some onto the point of his pen-knife, which he raised to his nostrils before sniffing. " Tar, I think, Watson. As is used on ships, would you not say ? " He held the knife towards me for my inspection.

I inhaled cautiously. " Tar of a certainty, but I would hesitate to identify it so precisely. What do you deduce from this ? "

" At present, nothing. Let us enter."

As soon as we passed into the hallway of the house, I was struck by a feeling that the house was far from being deserted. There was an indefinable air to the rooms that told me that they had recently been occupied by a number of people. Holmes, too, appeared to be aware of this, as he stood in the centre of the hallway, his keen senses strained.

" I am certain that you can sense it too," he said to me. " There is a faint, but distinct, smell of women's perfume, is there not ? And again that smell of tar."

I was unable to detect the odours to which Holmes was referring, but I followed him into one of the reception rooms at the rear of the house. The windows were covered by thick curtains, but it was possible to see in the gloom that the room was unfurnished, save for a large table, pushed against the wall and folded to take up as little space as possible. I moved to draw the curtain aside, but Holmes waved me back. " I would sooner leave this house as we found it, as far as is possible," he told me. " We know that it is occupied to serve some purpose for which there is some reason for concealment, and I would sooner not have those using it to know of our interest in the place." He stooped, and picked up a small round object, about one quarter of an inch in diameter, from the floor under the table.

" What is it ? " I asked.

" It would appear to be a sequin, of the type commonly adorning women's evening wear," he replied. " I am certain that this room was the centre of the activities that went on last night, whatever they may turn out to be. It is obvious that at least one of the women last night was here at some time." He continued to search through the room, and turned his attention to the folded table itself. " Now this, Watson, could prove to be of extreme importance," he exclaimed, suddenly straightening and holding something aloft. " This appeared to be wedged in the crack between the tabletop and the frame."

" I cannot see what it is that you are holding in this dim light," I complained.

" I will show you when we leave the house," he replied. " Let us make our way to the kitchen."

Downstairs in the basement kitchen, we were greeted by the sight of half a dozen empty bottles that had once contained champagne. " Nothing but the finest," remarked my friend, picking up one of these bottles, and examining the label. " And what do we have here ? " turning to another square bottle lying beside the champagne bottles. " Nothing more or less than Dutch *genever*, I do declare."

" But where are the glasses for the wine ? " I asked. It was a question that demanded an answer, for the kitchen was completely bare, other than the empty bottles that we had seen. An examination of the cupboards and the pantry yielded no clues.

" An excellent point," agreed Holmes. " It is hard to imagine the elegant society ladies whom we observed last night drinking from the bottle. Let us search the rest of the house."

Some time later, we were forced to admit defeat. Other than two pieces of tarred twine which we discovered in the passage leading to the rear of the house, and what I have already described, the house appeared to be completely empty. " It hardly seems natural for an empty house to contain as little as this," I said.

" It is indeed unnatural. The reason is that it is very carefully cleaned and emptied when it has been used for the purposes which we have yet to ascertain. This can be easily demonstrated by the pattern of the dust on the floor here and here, where it has obviously been brushed within the past few days."

As he spoke, a sound came from the back door as if a key was being turned in the lock.

" Quick ! Up the stairs as fast and as silently as you can manage ! " Holmes hissed at me, suiting his own actions to the words. I followed, and as I reached the landing on the first floor, I heard the door open, and the sound of two pairs of footsteps, and two deep male voices. I strained to make out the words, but was unable to distinguish what was being said, though the tone appeared to be angry, and strong words appeared to be passing between the two speakers. The footsteps appeared to descend the steps to the kitchen and returned a minute or two later, accompanied by the clink of glass. The sound of the back door opening, then closing, followed by the sound of a key in the lock, met our ears. We waited in silence for a few minutes, and then made our way down the stairs cautiously.

" I could not make out a word they were saying," I remarked to Holmes.

" For the excellent reason that they were not speaking English, and to the best of my knowledge you do not include proficiency in the Dutch tongue as one of your accomplishments," he retorted.

" Again, a Dutch connection ! "

" Indeed. Let us see if our Hollander friends, who by the sounds that we heard were responsible for removing the bottles that we discovered earlier, have left any traces of themselves behind them."

At the back door, which was locked, we encountered a temporary obstacle, which Holmes deftly overcame by methods which were, I regret to say, not those which should be in the compass of a law-abiding citizen. He then dropped to his knees, and examined the cinder-strewn path with his ever-present lens. " Square-toed boots of a peculiar pattern, typically that of a sea-boot," he remarked, after peering at some indentations, which appeared indistinct to me. " I think that at last I see some glimmering of light here."

I was still mystified, but assisted Holmes in refastening the door, and we left the house.

" What was it that you discovered in the table ? " I enquired.

For answer he passed me a red disc, about one-eighth of an inch thick, and about two inches in diameter, with the numeral " 5" emblazoned on it.

" This appears to be the kind of counter that is used as money in casinos and gaming-houses," I said.

" I am sure that is exactly what it is," replied Holmes. " The inference is therefore that by night, the house we have just visited changes its character, and becomes a casino for wealthy gamblers."

" So Lady Celia's guilty secret is that she is a gambler ? And she has been losing money, and selling the family treasures to pay the debts ? "

" I can think of few other alternative explanations. The question is, who is operating this little business, and how can they be prevented ? We can be certain that if Lady Celia has been driven to such extremities, she is not the only one. Who can tell what priceless *objets* have found their way into the hands of this gang, whoever they may be ? "

" It would seem likely that the gang is Dutch, though, would you not say ? "

" It is more than probable, I agree. And with the hints they have been kind enough to drop—the string, which was tarred, and tied in a knot that is peculiar to sailors, the footprint on the front step of the house, which deposited some tar, as used to caulk the decks of ships, and the imprint of a sea-boot on the path outside the back door, I think we can safely conclude that a ship is somehow involved in the carrying out of this business."

" In that case," I offered, after a few minutes' thought, " it would seem likely that the times at which Lady Celia and the others visit the house coincide with the times at which a particular Dutch ship visits London. The times when she stays at home are those when the ship is away, possibly at its home port."

Holmes stopped, and turned to face me. " Excellent, Watson ! I do believe that you have hit upon a significant part of the answer there. This now begins to make more sense than it did before. It would seem that the perpetrators set up the casino every night, leaving the house empty in the daytime."

" It would seem to me that such a plan would create pointless labour on their part, though."

" Not so. Consider that they are conducting operations that are certain to draw the attention of the authorities if they are made public. What better place to conduct them than in a house which is known to be empty ? There is, of course, the risk that the customers may be observed entering or leaving, but I would wager that the purpose of the carriage that we saw last night is to reduce the number of people who know about the operation, and to ensure that all entrances and exits are made when the visitors will be unobserved. Note that there are no houses opposite us, and this house is the end of the row, with the river on one side. It is hard to imagine a more perfect location for such a business in the centre of London."

" And since the house is known to be empty, it is unlikely to be suspected of harbouring any such activities ? " I suggested.

" Precisely so. And the beauty is that the place is open to anyone, such as ourselves, for inspection upon request and always appears to be completely innocent. What better way can you imagine to deflect any trace of suspicion ? "

" How would the apparatus needed for the casino be moved to and from the house on a regular basis ? " I asked.

" My belief is that we overlooked one or two hiding-places. I think we may assume that there will be some false floorboards, false backs to the cupboards, and the like, where furniture may be stored and produced only when it is needed. Ah, we are here again."

We had reached the offices of Johnstone, the agent, and we entered to return the key.

" Well ? " enquired Johnstone. " How do you like the place ? I must warn you again, that even if it does take your fancy, it is more than likely that Mr. de Vries will come up with some reason why you are not a suitable tenant."

" He need not rack his brain for excuses in this case," said Holmes. " I fear that it would be unsuitable for my needs. In any event, it would seem that a good deal of work would be necessary, especially as regards the interior, before I could even consider taking a lease."

" Do you really think so ? " replied the other. " It is strange that you should be of that opinion, because if I re-call correctly, the builders were called in to make renova-tions to the building only a little before Mr. de Vries placed the house on the market for letting."

" Well, well, that is my opinion only," replied Holmes equably. " I do not pretend to be an expert in these mat-ters, after all. Maybe I could have a word with the firm that carried out the work ? "

" Dear me, I am not sure that I can remember that."

Johnstone scratched his head, seemingly as an aid to memory. " Do you know, I cannot recall the name of the firm at all. Ah ! Now I remember. Mr. de Vries did not employ a local builder on that occasion, but used some Dutchmen who were in town at the time. Of course, it caused a small amount of bad feeling among the local tradesmen, who were of the opinion that their services should have been employed."

" I take it those Dutchmen are no longer in the neighbourhood ? "

" I never heard of them, save in connection with that work."

" No matter. In any case, I am grateful to you for the opportunity to see the house and for all the information that you have provided. However, in the event that I decide to change my mind, do you have an address at which I might reach Mr. de Vries ? "

" I am afraid that I am not at liberty to divulge such information," answered the agent. " My clients expect a certain amount of discretion in their business dealings with me."

" As do mine," agreed Holmes, introducing himself by name for the first time, to the surprise of the other.

" I see. Do you suspect Mr. de Vries of any criminal behaviour, then ? " he asked, obviously more than a little impressed by the name of the famous detective.

" No, it is nothing of that nature, believe me. I am simply curious as to the identity of the builders whom he employed. Though, as I said, the interior would require some work before I could even consider taking the place, there were one or two touches which, now that I come to consider it, definitely had a Dutch air to them. It would be pleasant if they could be reproduced at my brother's house in Kent."

" In that case, sir, here is the address which I use in my communications with Mr. de Vries." He passed a slip of paper to Holmes, who thanked him.

" And not a word of this to anyone, including Mr. de Vries, if you do not mind," Holmes told the agent. " In the event that I do not contact him about the builders, it would worry him unnecessarily, do you not agree, if he were to learn that a detective had been on his trail." He smiled at Johnstone, tipping his hat, and we left the offices.

" The Dutch builders were constructing hiding places for the casino apparatus and furniture ? " I asked.

" One must assume so. There would seem to be little advantage in importing builders from overseas otherwise, would there ? "

" So you will watch Mr. de Vries, now that you have his address ? "

" No, I will reserve that task for you. I want you to stay outside his house and follow him wherever he may go to-night. I will follow the carriage carrying the patrons of the gaming-house, and mark its destination or destinations when Lady Celia and her companions return from there. Discovering the identity of these others will be another significant step in solving the case."

Accordingly, that evening I placed myself in a convenient location opposite the house in Chalk Farm that we had been told was that of de Vries, where I could watch the house without myself being seen. I had a cab standing by around the corner, ready to carry me should de Vries decide to use that method of transport.

It was a cold evening, and I found myself stamping and rubbing my gloved hands together in an attempt to maintain the circulation in my extremities. I had no idea how long I was to have to wait. Holmes had instructed me that I should call off my vigil at midnight if there was no sign of any activity before then. Added to my problems was the fact that I had no description of de Vries. Holmes had earlier dispatched Wiggins, one of the gang of urchins whom he had dubbed " The Baker-street Irregulars", with a message for Mr. de Vries, to be delivered personally, and instructions that the appearance of de Vries was to be reported to him and me, in order to aid me in my identification. However, in the event, Wiggins had been unable to deliver the message as requested, and had therefore been unable to furnish a description.

My patience was rewarded at about half past eight, when a tall thin figure, heavily bearded and apparently wearing a long opera cloak with a tall silk hat, emerged from the house, and made its way to a carriage which had drawn out of a side-street.

I rushed back to my waiting hansom, and instructed the driver, whom I had previously promised a generous payment, to follow the other carriage at a discreet distance. We set off at a slow pace, keeping about a hundred yards between ourselves and our quarry. Occasionally we lost sight of him, but by quickening the pace a little, it was possible to keep on his trail. The route he followed was somewhat confusing, though. At first I had imagined that we would be heading for the house in Finsbury which Holmes and I had visited earlier in the day, but at Holloway, we took an unexpected road to the right, rather than the left turn I had been anticipating, and headed south down the Holloway-road, turning right again at Islington and proceeding towards Kings Cross, from where we turned again, finishing our journey at Chalk Farm where we had started. It seemed possible to me that de Vries would make another sortie later that evening, and so I waited until midnight, the time I had agreed with Holmes, but in vain, as no figure emerged from the house during the time that I stood in the cold street.

Somewhat chagrined at my experience, I instructed the driver to carry me back to Baker-street, where I awaited the return of Sherlock Holmes. I poured myself a brandy and soda, and devoured two or three of the roast beef sandwiches that Mrs. Hudson had left for us. Although I had fully intended to stay awake to greet Holmes on his return, the warmth of the fire, coupled with the effects of my refreshment, caused me to fall asleep. I woke to become aware that Holmes was in the room, standing in front of the fire, a sandwich in his hand, smiling down at me.

" By Jove, it is cold outside, is it not ? I am chilled to the marrow."

" What time is it ? " I asked him.

" About a half after three. I can guess you had poor hunting, and returned a little after midnight."

I confirmed this deduction. " I was taken round in a circle, returning to the place where I had started," I complained.

" No doubt he had spotted you and your carriage, and took appropriate action. In the event, he never made an appearance at the Finsbury house that I could observe."

" But others did, I take it, judging by the lateness of your return ? "

" Indeed so." Here Holmes named three prominent Society ladies, other than Lady Celia, whose names I shall not repeat here. " Though all wore domino masks, I believe that I am correct in my identification, since I was standing considerably closer to the house than were we on the previous occasion. As you may know, there are many more ways to identify an individual than by their facial features alone. There are certain peculiarities of posture and gait that are often more revealing than a face, and these are figures who are very much in the public eye. "

" Do you believe that these women too, have fallen into this trap, and have been forced to sell the family treasures ? "

" It is impossible to tell at this stage," he replied. " I strongly suspect, however, that the gambling den being operated will not be honest, and that it will be impossible for any gambler to win. There are many such ways in which such an establishment can be operated in such a way as to turn a tidy profit for its owners. There are tales of roulette wheels with hidden braking mechanisms to be operated by the croupier, as well as the more usual stratagems of marked cards and loaded dice that are often used to gull the frequenters of such places. If this is the case here, then we can be assured that the gamblers we have seen tonight will have suffered losses, possibly on the same scale as Lady Celia, forcing them to dispose of their family heirlooms surreptitiously."

" How can you discover whether this is the case ? " I asked him.

" I have yet to decide the precise method." He yawned mightily. " Come, Watson, it is time that we sought the comfort of our beds for the night. We will ponder these matters at more length in the morning."

Although I considered myself to have rested only merely adequately when I arose at a relatively early hour the next morning, Holmes was already awake, breakfasting, albeit unshaven and in his dressing-gown.

" May I trouble you to bring over the newspapers, which

I may assume that Mrs. Hudson, not wishing to offend my modesty, has left outside the door ? "

I brought the journals to the table, and passed the *Times* to him, whereupon he commenced scanning the agony column, as was his habit, while I perused the society pages of the *Morning Post*. An item therein caught my eye, and I exclaimed aloud.

" Holmes, you told me, did you not, that the Duchess of _____shire was one of the party that you followed last night, did you not ? "

" I did."

" Are you certain it was she whom you observed ? "

" My dear man, I may not follow these matters with the same devotion as do you, but Her Grace is a well-known and distinctive figure. It could have been none other that I saw last night. Why do you ask ? "

" She is reported here as having attended a function at the Worshipful Company of Glovers, from eight in the evening until midnight."

The expression on Holmes' face changed, as he fairly snatched the newspaper from my hands and read the article with his own eyes. " I am certain I am not mistaken in my identification," he protested. " It is time for us to visit the offices of this journal at the earliest possible opportunity." So saying, he downed the remainder of his coffee, and disappeared to his bedroom, from which he emerged some time later, shaved and attired for the day.

" You are ready ? " he asked me.

I in my turn swallowed my coffee, and followed him out of the house, from where we hailed a cab to take us to the *Post*'s offices. Once there, Holmes demanded the identity of the article's author of the sub-editor to whom we had been referred.

" That would be Oliver Ripley," we were informed.

" And where is his desk ? " asked Holmes.

The newspaperman laughed in my friend's face. " My dear sir, Ripley has no permanent position in this office. He attends the functions he describes in his reports, and sends us his copy by messenger. We hardly see him in here from one month's end to the next."

" Very good. Where will I find him ? "

Again, a mocking laugh was the initial reply to this question. " In bed, I would imagine, at this hour. Our Mr. Ripley is something of a night owl."

" And his bed would be where, exactly ? "

The other sensed Holmes' irritation and the fact that he was, with some difficulty, keeping his temper in check, and modified his tone. " He lives in Hampstead," he told us, and scribbled an address on a card. " But be warned, he may not be at his most communicative at this hour."

Holmes took the card, and we took a cab to the address in Hampstead, which turned out to be a lodging house off Rosslyn Hill.

The landlady who opened the door to us examined Holmes' card, and informed us shortly that Ripley was not available.

" I heard him come in at four this morning," she told us, with a sniff. " And somewhat the worse for drink, I would say, judging by the noise he made going up the stairs."

" Maybe we could enquire at his door ? " suggested Holmes.

" You can do that by all means," she retorted, " but I wouldn't expect any results from him at only half-past ten in the morning. Third on the left on the second floor."

" Thank you, Mrs. Greenslade," replied Holmes, leaving

the good woman, as well as myself, puzzled as to how he knew her name.

" How— ? " I asked as we panted up the stairs.

" Did you fail to notice the note to the baker's boy signed by Mrs. Emily Greenslade outside the front door ? No ? There are times when I positively despair of you, Watson," he replied. " Never mind, we are here." He rapped smartly on the door with his knuckles.

After the third bout of knocking there was a reply from within the room.

" Curse you, whoever you may be, and go away," were the words, uttered in a muffled tone.

Holmes repeated his tattoo on the door.

" Are you _____ deaf ? I told you to go away. You can give me the money tomorrow," came the answer, a little more clearly this time.

" Well ? " said Holmes quietly to me, raising his eye-brows, and knocked once more. This time, more definite results were forthcoming. We heard the sound of slippered feet moving towards the door, which was flung open to re-veal a middle-aged man, dressed in night attire, with a startled expression on his face, and his tousled hair stick-ing from his head at all angles. He regarded Holmes and myself in seeming astonishment.

" You're not Sir Godfrey, are you ? " he said in surprise.

" I believe not," said my friend, smiling. " And neither is my colleague here."

" Then who the deuce are you ? "

" My name is Sherlock Holmes. Maybe you have heard of me ? "

" The detective fellow, eh ? What do you want at this unearthly hour ? I was up late last night."

" So Mrs. Greenslade informed us just now. I merely

wish to know where you went last night after the function at the Glovers'."

" How did you know I was there ? " The sleep-filled eyes appeared to narrow as he attempted to concentrate on Holmes' face.

" Your editor, Mr. Plumley, at the *Post* informed us that you had written the piece describing the function."

" What's it to you where I was and what I was doing ? If you want to know, I left that group of toffs and took myself to a cabman's shelter near Charing Cross which I sometimes use when I have copy to write late at night. It's warm, and they're a good crowd. Half a bottle of whisky provides me with company, warmth and a place to write, and when shared generously enough, sometimes one of the drivers will even take my copy to be delivered to the office. I then returned here by cab. Now, is that enough for you, Mr. Nosy-Parker ? Or is there anything else you wish to know ? "

" No, that will be sufficient, Mr. Ripley. Thank you. I am sorry to have disturbed your slumbers."

We turned and made our way down the stairs, thanking Mrs. Greenslade on our way out of the house.

" I told you that you were wasting your time there," she told us, with a certain self-satisfaction.

" And you were perfectly correct, dear lady," replied Holmes. " Thank you all the same." He made a courtly bow, and we let ourselves into the street, where we walked to the Hill, and turned the corner, before Holmes broke into an unrestrained chuckle. " The cleverness of the man. He gives us an alibi which is no alibi, and yet..."

" How do you mean ? "

" Consider, Watson. What time did the function finish,

according to the report in the *Post*, which, let us remember, was written by Ripley himself ? "

" At eleven," I said.

" Let us allow him some fifteen minutes to reach his cabman's shelter, some thirty minutes to write his copy—it was after all a short piece consisting largely of names—and then another ten minutes for the copy to reach the *Post*. That would provide ample time for editing and setting the piece."

" So you think his work was completed before midnight ? "

" Well before midnight. Why, then, would it take him four hours to return to Hampstead from Charing Cross, especially as he was in the easiest place in the world from which to hail a cab ? "

" I cannot conceive that it could take so long."

" Nor I. We must therefore conclude that he returned to Hampstead via another route, such as one which took him through Finsbury."

" For what purpose ? "

" To mark who was in attendance at the house there, and to provide alibis for them. Let us assume that he marked the attendance in Finsbury, wrote his piece there, and sent it to Fleet-street by a messenger. How often have you heard it asserted that a fact must be true because it has been printed in a newspaper ? "

" Often enough," I admitted.

" So given that the ladies whom I observed last night are reported as having attended a social function, who would question the facts as reported ? "

" The others who attended, perhaps ? "

" Given the press of guests at these events, it is often impossible to determine who is there and who is not. Could any of those who were actually present at last night's gathering swear that Lady Celia, for example, was or was not present ? I very much doubt it."

" The husbands or partners of the other ladies whom you observed ? " I suggested.

" I would wager that they are all out of Town at present, as is Sir Godfrey. Let me correct myself. I believed Sir Godfrey to be out of Town, and yet Ripley appeared to be expecting a visit from him. Can we assume, therefore, that Sir Godfrey is still in this city, unknown to all but a few ? I think so," answering himself.

" And Ripley just now was expecting to be paid by him for some service ? "

" That is the inference that I, too made, based on his words. Deep waters here, Watson, deep waters."

" What does it all mean ? "

" What this means, Watson, is that a line of enquiry that I had considered pursuing is now closed to me."

" Your plan was to use the newspaper reports that I had previously researched to check on the attendance of those whom you suspected of being present at these gambling sessions ? "

" Precisely, Watson. You know my methods in these matters all too well, do you not ? Now we can be reasonably certain that these reports are not to be trusted. Let it be a lesson to you. What is printed in the Press all too often serves the interests of those responsible for its writing, and does not always serve the cause of truth."

" So we are back where we started ? " I cried in despair.

" Hardly. I now have a list of three in addition to Lady Celia whom we suspect of having lost money at the casino, and whom, I guess, will have disposed of heirlooms—paintings or jewellery or some such—in order to meet the debts they have incurred. Our task, Watson, is not first and foremost to recover such items, but to prevent this business from continuing. What do we know so far ? " Holmes started to tick off points on his fingers as we walked along. " First, we may reasonably assume a connection with the Netherlands, may we not ? There seems to be a Dutch connection at every turn."

" Including the van Dyck painting which you were examining," I added.

" By Jove, Watson ! That is correct. I wonder if any other artworks or heirlooms that may have been disposed of or substituted in the same manner also have such a connection ? "

" The diamonds that Sir Godfrey mentioned to you ? "

" There may well be a connection with the Amsterdam diamond trade, of course. If we are to examine the possessions of these families, I am confident that we will discover a Dutch connection in all the cases.

" The second point of which I am aware is that these women are all married to significantly older husbands, as far as I am aware. I will be interested to discover under what circumstances the couples first met each other."

" You suspect something ? "

" Gambling, Watson, is not a habit that comes to one of a sudden, at least not on the scale that we suspect here. My belief is that these women have a history of frequenting casinos, and of partaking in games of chance, and I would be hardly surprised were it to transpire that they met their future husbands at a watering place such as Monte Carlo or Deauville."

" Come, this is something of a strain on the imagination."

" Nonetheless," he replied, seemingly a little nettled, " I

would be much astonished should none of these marriages prove to have originated under such circumstances."

" I am guessing that you wish me to investigate the matter ? " My words were half in jest, but Sherlock Holmes took me at my word.

" I believe that this type of matter is more in your line than mine," he replied. " Maybe you can renew your acquaintance with the estimable Mr. Plumley at the *Post*. I am sure that he will be delighted to let you look through the files of the reports relating to such matters."

" And meanwhile, how will you be engaged ? "

" I shall be making discreet enquiries related to the works of art and so on owned by the families of those whom I observed last night in Finsbury. I think we may be sure that we will find a common thread there, related to the Netherlands."

I have to confess that the thought of searching through many years of society pages did not fill me with any great sense of anticipation. I foresaw many weary hours of searching through dusty files attempting to locate and pick out a few nuggets of gold from a pile of useless ore.

However, the task proved to be significantly easier than I had feared. Plumley, the editor to whom we had spoken earlier, informed me that an ingenious system of filing, using numbered tags, would allow me to search easily for the details of the three ladies whom Holmes had observed. He enquired of me how we had fared on our expedition to Hampstead, but I was as non-committal on the subject as I felt was possible without overstepping the bounds of politeness.

In the event, it took me a little more than three hours to discover what I needed to know, rather than the three days or even longer that I had been expecting. When I returned to Baker-street bearing the fruits of my labours in my notebook, it was with a certain sense of triumph. Sherlock Holmes was fulsome in his congratulations.

" You have surpassed yourself, Watson," he told me. " I certainly was not expecting such a speedy and complete result. So," throwing himself into his favourite armchair and stretching out his arms above his head, " tell me all that you have discovered."

" It is exactly as you prophesied," I replied. " In every case, the happy couple commenced their acquaintanceship at a watering place in which a casino is located. Monte Carlo, as you surmised, and one or two others in France. By the by, I do not think that I deserve credit for the speed of my researches." I proceeded to provide Holmes with an account of the system used at the newspaper, to which he listened with interest.

" A system which would definitely appear to be of value," he commented. " One day, when there is no urgent press of business, it may be of some interest for me to reorganise my Index along the lines that you have just described."

" And what of your researches ? " I asked him.

He smiled ruefully, and shook his head. " I regret to say that they have not proceeded at the same speed as did yours. I have, however, ascertained that in at least two cases a valuable work by a Dutch Old Master is hanging on the walls. There does indeed appear to be some kind of connection."

" I can understand why you are reluctant to call in the police, since the exposure of these activities would undoubtedly cause a great scandal in society. But I see no reason why we should not in some sense take the law into our own hands and put a stop to this business ourselves."

Sherlock Holmes folded his hands behind his head once

more and looked at me steadily. " I can hardly believe what I am hearing," he said to me, smiling. " Is this the John Watson that I know, the defender of law and order ? You are now proposing an act which would put us beyond the law ? "

I could feel the blood rushing to my cheeks as I responded. " It would not be the first time that such has occurred," I reminded him. " Do you not believe that there are times when such action is justified ? "

" You know very well that I am prepared to overlook the niceties of our legal system from time to time. However, I feel that at the present moment it would be premature for us to act in this matter. We could certainly, as you suggest, put a stop to the operations of this gang, at least insofar as the gambling house is concerned. We could possibly even prevent them permanently from restarting the scheme. It would seem unlikely, though, that we could trace either the missing artworks, or the mastermind who has organised this operation. I need time, and data, before proceeding further."

" There is one aspect of this matter which I do not understand," I said. " We know that there are nights when Sir Godfrey is not in Town, but Lady Celia does not go to gamble. What is the reason for this ? "

" I can think of many reasons," he replied. " For example, she may have no access to ready cash or even to the credit that she needs to make her bets on the cards or dice or roulette wheel or whatever game of chance is played there. It may be that the husbands of her companions are in London, and they are unable to join her, and the gang feel that it is not in their interests to open up the establishment for one or two gamblers alone. There may be a minimum number of customers, for want of a better term, below which the game is not worth the candle. As a third explanation, I might offer the idea that the true master of the operation is not in London continually, and that the casino only operates when he is present. Indeed, now I come to consider the matter more fully, I feel that this last explanation is the true one."

" How is that ? "

" There must be some method for the gang to remove the valuable items which they have received—the paintings and so on out of the country to Holland. That is, of course, if our assumptions regarding the ultimate destination of these works of art are correct. Since the items in question are of a very high value—indeed, in the case of the paintings we can say that they are priceless—I consider it to be unlikely that they would be entrusted to mere minions. The leader of the gang would wish to take personal charge of them. We were discussing the possibility of a ship's being involved a few days ago, were we not, and I now believe that this is the solution to the conundrum. De Vries is travelling back and forth between the two countries on a ship, and while he is in Holland, the gaming-house does not operate."

" I follow your reasoning, but fail to see how this helps us. Do you now believe that this Mr. de Vries is that leader ? "

" It is possible. Bear in mind, though, that we have yet to ascertain whether he resides permanently in London or not. However, that is a relatively easy matter to settle. I venture to suggest that if he is known to come and go, and the periods of his presence in London coincide with the activities of the house in Finsbury, we can confidently assert that he is indeed the leader, at least for this end of the business."

" Then the matter is easily solved ! " I exclaimed.

" In a highly unsatisfactory manner," retorted Holmes.
" The method of deduction that I have just described,
though it would almost certainly lead to a correct conclusion regarding the gang and its leadership, would require
much time and effort before we could be certain of its success or failure. No, as I see it we have two courses of action
open to us. The first of these is one that you mentioned
earlier—that we call in the police and we put a stop, even
if only temporary, to the activities of this gang. But I fear
that de Vries, if indeed he is the leader, would undoubtedly
slip through the police net and continue his activities elsewhere at some other time. We have seen already that he is
a cautious man, and is not without a certain cunning in
his operations."

" And the other course of action that you are
considering ? "

" Is simply to continue what we have been doing. That
is to say, keeping watch on the house in Finsbury as well as
on de Vries. I suggest that tonight we reverse our roles. I
wish you to keep an eye on the house, and I will attempt to
follow our Mr. de Vries, though from what you say he may
prove to be a somewhat more slippery fish than others we
have followed in the past."

I prepared myself for another cold night of watching and
waiting. Holmes had instructed me to wait outside the
house until any visitors had departed, and I therefore paid
off my hansom cab some distance away from the house and
walked the last two hundred yards or so to the same place
where Holmes and I had previously kept watch. As I waited, I observed the same carriage as previously pull up, and
four female figures alight from it, one of which was carrying a flat square package, of about two feet on a side. As

Holmes had mentioned to me, all appeared to be wearing some kind of mask which hid their faces, but at least two of the party were recognisable by me, even in the darkness. As before, they ascended the steps to the front door, which was opened from within, and the carriage pulled away as they entered the building. A dim light was visible in the fanlight above the door, and even this was soon extinguished, giving the impression that the house was unoccupied. I settled myself down as comfortably as I could in the shadow of a tree on the far side of the road, and found myself hoping that the road did not lie on the beat of a policeman, since I did not relish the prospect of explaining my presence to an officer of the law. I believe that I only remained awake, for I was deathly tired, on account of this concern regarding my questioning and even possibly my arrest. I dared not smoke, for fear that the lighting of a match or the glow of tobacco might alert others to my presence, despite the heavy night mist that was thickening almost visibly. I therefore stood huddled in my overcoat, silently shivering, alone with my thoughts. I was startled out of my reverie by a heavy hand on my shoulder, almost causing me to jump in the air with fright. I whirled around, ready to face my attacker.

" Not so fast, Watson," hissed a well-known voice." I am delighted to see that you are still awake, at any rate."

" Holmes ! " I ejaculated. " How long have you been here ? "

" Quiet," he admonished me. " Though we can be reasonably certain that no one is listening, it behoves us to take no unnecessary risks in this matter. I have been here for the last half hour at least, amusing myself by watching your fidgeting. I observed a certain drowsiness in your manner, and determined that you should not sleep." I could see his teeth flash white in the darkness as he smiled at me.

" Then de Vries has not come here ? " I asked.

" On the contrary. I followed him here."

" I have seen no-one enter the house other than the patrons of the establishment, if I may term them so. How could he have arrived ? " I objected.

" He is, as we had suspected, not without some cunning aspects to his nature. He did not enter the house by the back door. Indeed, his carriage never even entered this road, but took a route behind the house, stopping by the river. He walked along the path by the side of the river and let himself into the house through the back door. I have every expectation that he will use the same route for his return, so let us wait for him at the point where his carriage dropped him earlier tonight. On the other night when he led you that little dance around the streets of London, I have little doubt that he slipped out of the back door of the Chalk Farm house and made his way to Finsbury, where he used the same method of entry as tonight."

I followed Holmes by the side of the house along the riverbank until we came to another road.

" This is where the carriage dropped him earlier, and from where I expect him to make his departure. We will wait here. Did you observe anything of interest this evening ? "

I informed Holmes of the package that I had seen carried by one of the ladies who had entered the house.

" Do you feel that this could be a work of art ? " he asked me.

" It is perfectly possible."

" In which case, I consider it absolutely essential that we follow him away from here tonight. If he is in possession of a priceless work of art, I think it is unlikely that he will wish to keep it in his house, and he will feel it necessary to take it out of the country as soon as possible. This may be the vital element that leads to the satisfactory resolution of this case. It is essential, though, that he be totally unaware of our presence." He pulled out his watch and announced the time without so much as a glance at its face. " If events proceed as they have in the past, I estimate that we have less than an hour to wait."

I could not contain my curiosity, and asked him how he had been able to ascertain the hour in the dark, without even looking at his watch.

" On occasions like this, I carry a timepiece which has been adapted for the needs of the blind, whereby the crystal can be lifted on a hinge, allowing my fingers to feel the position of the hands. It is invaluable under the kind of circumstances in which we find ourselves at present, when it is necessary to remain unobserved. But hark ! What do we have here ? "

As he spoke, I perceived a carriage making its way towards us through the mist. " It is the carriage that de Vries used ? "

" Assuredly. Excellently spotted, Watson. Yes, indeed, it is stopped now in the same place where de Vries left it."

" How do you propose to follow him ? "

" Our cab is waiting around the corner. As before, when we see our mark, I want you to alert the driver, and come with the cab to where I am waiting. We will then follow at a discreet distance, though I fear at this time of night it will be difficult to trace our quarry unobserved."

It was no warmer than it had been, and my self-control was stretched to the limits to prevent me from stamping my feet to keep them warm. However, the knowledge that

Holmes was by my side was at once a comfort to me and a spur to my determination to stay awake. It was I who first spotted a tall figure, dressed in an opera cloak and wearing a silk hat, making its way along the riverside to the waiting carriage. As it approached closer, I observed the beard which I had seen the previous night, and noted that a package, seemingly the same that I had observed earlier being carried by one of the female patrons of the casino, was tucked under its arm. I pointed out the apparition to Holmes.

" Yes, it is he," he whispered. " Go now, and alert the cabbie."

I moved swiftly and as unobtrusively as I was able to the spot that Holmes had earlier indicated to me where our conveyance was waiting, and instructed the driver to move off slowly and silently. We had gone a few yards before it came to me that a familiar sound—that of the horse's hoofs—was absent, and the rattle of the wheels that is usually associated with this mode of transport was likewise missing. As we passed the point where I had left homes waiting, we slackened our pace a little, and Holmes joined me in the carriage, without our having stopped. I remarked on the relative silence of our journey.

" I provided our driver, whom I have used on several similar occasions before this, in advance with instructions and the necessary resources to make our travel as silent as possible. Maybe the mist and fog that have so providentially appeared would hide us from sight, but in streets as nearly deserted as this, the sound of another vehicle would carry and would alert our friend. A few bags of bran tied around the feet of the horse, and a little careful lubrication of the wheels and springs of the cab, appear to have worked wonders, do they not ? "

I agreed, and peered out of the windows to determine our direction of travel.

Holmes noticed my interest. " If my suppositions are correct, we are heading towards the docks. I hardly think that he will wish to keep this painting or drawing, or whatever it may prove to be, in the country for longer than is necessary, and he would be foolish to take the risk of transporting it on a public ferry."

It appeared that once again Sherlock Holmes had deduced correctly. A little before the dock area, the carriage that we were following stopped, and its passenger descended. Homes immediately rapped on the roof of our vehicle, signalling to the driver to halt. " Do not bother to wait," he instructed our cabbie, passing him a number of coins. " You have done a good job tonight, and I may require your services once again in the near future. I will be in contact. When you leave, ensure that you are not seen by the carriage that we have been following. I expect it to turn and return to the centre of Town very soon."

" Just as you say, Mr. Holmes," replied the driver, touching his hat as he started his uncannily silent hansom cab on the journey home.

" Now, Watson," Holmes said to me softly. " Keep to the shadows, and do your best to keep silent."

Even in the dim light, it was easy to distinguish our quarry as he walked towards the quayside where a small tramp steamer was moored. At its stern fluttered an ensign, which I recognised as that of the kingdom of the Netherlands. De Vries made straight for the ship, and we could see now that he was carrying the package with him. He walked up the gangplank onto the deck of the ship, where he was met and greeted by a man who was presumably a member of the ship's crew, and the gang-plank was immediately drawn up after him.

" I was not expecting to see things as well-prepared as this," muttered Holmes. On the stern of the boat, we could read the name *Friesland*, followed by the name of the ship's home port, Rotterdam. " A name we will do well to remember," Holmes said to me in a low voice.

We turned away from the dock, powerless to make any move against the ship or its crew. " Do you know the identity of the woman who carried the package into the house this evening ? " Holmes asked me.

" From the list of those that you observed the other night, I would have to say that it is the Duchess."

" I agree with you. I believe that the Duke has in his possession—or what now seems to be more likely, used to have in his possession—a Rembrandt drawing which is said to be one of the finest of its type in the entire world. It is my belief that the package we have seen carried onto the ship just now represents the original of one of the choicest examples of the master's draughtsmanship. I happen to know that the Duke is at present in Norfolk, and I shall run down there tomorrow. I will also pay a visit on Sir Godfrey, whose country seat is near to that of the Duke, and I shall acquaint him with our progress so far. While I am doing that, I wish you to make enquiries as to the identity of the owner of that ship and discover all that you can of its comings and goings. When we return to Baker-Street I will give you the card of one of the clerks in the Port Office who has been of service to me in the past. He will require his palm to be greased, but I anticipate full recompense from Sir Godfrey, and possibly the Duke also, for any expenses that may be incurred in this regard. A couple of sovereigns should suffice in this case." He broke off. " My dear fellow, are you cold ? "

" More than a little." In truth, I was chilled to the marrow. " I fear that I may be catching a chill, or worse, if I stay outside for much longer."

" My apologies. I was so consumed with the thrill of the chase that bodily discomfort was the furthest thing from my mind. Happily we have been deposited in an area of London where I have friends. Follow me."

The acquaintances of Sherlock Holmes never failed to fill me with amazement, both in their number and in their variety. Holmes led me a short distance from the docks, to an establishment seemingly operated for the benefit of the dock labourers and sailors, which served hearty fare in the form of hot soup and baked potatoes, which appeared to be the only items on the menu. I hesitated before entering, but Holmes showed no such worries, and made his way to the counter as if he were a regular customer. To my astonishment, the proprietor greeted him by name.

" A cold night, Mr. Holmes."

" It is indeed, Jim. Two large bowls of your finest, and two large potatoes." He pushed some silver across the counter, which I estimated to be more than ample for the food he had just ordered. " And may I introduce my colleague, Dr. Watson here," gesturing towards me.

" Pleased to make your acquaintance, sir," said the man referred to as ' Jim'. " I've heard Mr. Holmes here talk of you many times, and tell me that if it were not for you he could not do his work."

I glanced at Holmes, whose face was now set in a sort of half-smile. He nodded at me and caught my eye. At that moment I felt the strength of the bond between us which was rarely expressed, except at moments like this. Two steaming bowls of soup were placed in front of us, and I can honestly say that I have hardly ever enjoyed any food so much in my life.

As we finished the soup, Jim placed a plate with a baked potato and a pat of butter in front of each of us, and we fell to. " Excellent as always, Jim," Holmes remarked. " Maybe there's something else you can provide for us ? " He leaned forward, and the other copied the gesture, so that their faces were less than a foot apart over the table. They spoke in low voices.

" What do you know of that Dutch tramp, the *Friesland* ? "

" You mean the one that's tied up at the docks down there ? " Jim jerked a thumb over his shoulder.

" That is the one I mean."

" She's an odd one, and no mistake. Three times in as many months she's just taken off in the middle of the night. No word of goodbye, no pilot. Now if she was running stuff into the country, I could understand her coming in and tying up without anyone noticing, but it doesn't make any sense for her to be setting off like that all the time. You know," scratching his head, " I don't know as I have ever seen her set sail in the daylight. She's a bit of a night bird, that one."

" Do any of her crew ever come in here ? "

" Hard to tell. We get all sorts in here. Wait, though. Yes, I remember two of them coming in once. Spoke quite good English. Didn't think much of my soup, as I recall. You know, there's something else funny about the *Friesland*. She's often here for three or four days at a time, but I hardly ever see anyone loading stuff onto her or taking stuff off her. Is there something strange going on there, can you tell me ? "

" I do not believe there is anything untoward." He added, as if it were an afterthought, " Just to be on the safe side, will you get word to me the next time she calls in port ? "

" It will be a pleasure, Mr. Holmes."

We left the restaurant (for so I suppose I must term it) and set off for the main road in search of transport to return us to Baker-street. " I may assume that your lack of interest in the *Friesland* is indeed pretended ? " I said to Holmes.

" Naturally. I have no wish to attract more attention than is necessary. I have used Jim as a source of information on a number of occasions following his release from gaol, where he had been confined following a wrongful conviction for burglary—you recall the Bishopsgate jewel case ? —which I was able to overturn, and secure his release. While he is from time to time a very valuable resource to me in my work, he does suffer from a failing in that he tends to overindulge, and has been known to let slip various pieces of information which would better have remained hidden from the common gaze, so to speak." We walked on in silence for a while. Suddenly, Holmes addressed me. " This is going to be a rough business, Watson. I feel there is more at risk here than your simply catching a cold. There is, I believe, a very real chance of my perishing in the attempt to stop this business, and you with me, should you persist in your folly in accompanying me in this business."

" How can you say such a thing ? " I asked Holmes. " In any event, whether or not the business is dangerous, you can count on my being at your side for as long as you need me there."

" Have no fear. I do not doubt your courage or your

loyalty for an instant, but I do wish to make you fully aware of the danger into which you may be running. I have reason to believe that de Vries may be more deeply connected with European criminal organisations than I first suspected. My connections do not run to the Dutch police force, however, but I have telegraphed my friend in the French detective service, Monsieur Le Villard, to enquire if he has any information regarding this matter. He is rapidly gaining a reputation for his successes which, if I may be permitted my moment of vanity, is due at least in part to the hints I have been able to pass to him on various subjects. He is well aware of the debt he owes me, and I expect an answer to arrive at Baker-street in the next few hours at most. Ah ! You have no objection to an omnibus ? " Indeed, dawn was breaking, and the morning fogs were disappearing as the metropolis woke to the life of a new day.

We caught the omnibus that Holmes had espied and eventually arrived at Baker-street, where Mrs. Hudson presented Holmes with a telegram.

" Just come this moment, Mr. Holmes," she said. " I was going to take it up to you, not knowing that you and the Doctor were out. I'm sure you'd both like a nice cup of tea ? "

" Coffee, if you would be so kind, Mrs. Hudson. Strong, black, and plenty of it."

" And for you, Doctor ? "

" Doctor Watson will have the same," replied Holmes, before I could answer. " We will need to be alert today. Remember, I am for Norfolk, and you are for the Port Office. That reminds me." He reached into a pigeonhole of his desk, and extracted a card which he handed to me.

Loudon is your man. You have sufficient funds ? " I replied in the affirmative.

Following two cups of some of the strongest coffee I have ever imbibed, and a few rounds of toast, Holmes and I set off on our respective errands. Once I had located the clerk Loudon, and the financial obligations consequent on doing business with him had been met, it proved a relatively simple matter for him to give me the dates on which the *Friesland* had called at the port.

" The times here are not exact, mark you," he warned me. " She seems to come and go much as she pleases, without a pilot. But I can tell you that the dates are correct, because she pays her wharfage fees for the days she's here. And if she didn't, there'd be trouble, I can tell you."

I wrote down the list of dates in my notebook.

" Anything else you want to know ? "

Though Holmes had not specifically asked for the information, I thought it worthwhile to enquire what sort of cargo had been declared, and with whom the shipping company did business.

" That wouldn't be our affair," I was told. " It might be possible to find out if you really wanted to know. I had heard a rumour that they were running things into Holland that they shouldn't be doing. It's none of our business here in this country, of course, if they want to buy good Scotch whisky and take it to the Dutchmen there without their Customs knowing about it. Of course, if they were running Dutch gin here without paying the duty, that would be a different matter."

I thanked him, and armed with this knowledge, returned to Baker-street to await Sherlock Holmes. In the event, I had not long to wait.

" Excellent ! " said he upon entering. " Have the

goodness to ring for Mrs. Hudson. I am famished, and I have a fancy for buttered eggs or some such." Our house-keeper entered, and Holmes placed his order.

" You said matters were excellent ? " I enquired, when Mrs. Hudson had departed.

" For us, yes. Our supposition is correct. Maybe things are not so excellent for His Grace, but I was not so *gauche* as to inform him of that fact. The Rembrandt drawing in his London town house which he was kind enough to let me examine is undoubtedly a modern copy. I went to vis-it him in Norfolk, and informed him, since he recognised my name, that I had been retained by an insurance com-pany to check one or two details, including the drawing in question. He thereupon provided me with a letter of intro-duction, which I handed to the butler of the London house on my return to Town, and I was left alone with the so-called Rembrandt. A palpable fake, my dear Watson. The paper, the medium in which the drawing was executed— all demonstrably modern. The execution, however, was competent."

" If you ever succeed in putting the criminal element of London out of business altogether," I laughed, " you will have another trade on which you may fall back."

" I doubt if it will ever come to that pass," he replied, " but it is a pleasant enough fancy, to be sure."

" And Sir Godfrey ? " I asked.

" I had taken the precaution of telegraphing in advance, and received a reply informing me that he would not be in residence. No reason was given. Accordingly, I did not bother to pay a visit. And how did you fare ? " he asked me.

I told him of what I had discovered, and he listened with interest. " The idea of smuggling whisky seems to be an ingenious one. If they were ever caught, they could give up the whisky casks, receive a nominal punishment, and no exciseman would ever dream of investigating further. The trick of hiding a larger crime behind a smaller one is one that I have observed before. The Grotton affair was before your time, but that was an excellent example of the stratagem."

" What is our next move ? Are we simply going to wait for the *Friesland* to come here again ? "

" No. I think we will pay another visit to Finsbury, now we have a clearer idea of what we seek."

" You propose to bother the house-agent once more ? "

" I do not think we will trouble him on this occasion," smiled Holmes. " I am sorry to turn your night into day once more, but I feel a nocturnal expedition will yield more satisfactory results. Provided, as always, that you wish to accompany me."

" Holmes ! " I exclaimed in irritation that was only partially feigned. " I am by now becoming seriously annoyed at these repeated references of yours, suggesting that I am unwilling to assist you." I attempted to adopt an expression of ferocity, but the effort proved too much, and I burst out in a fit of laughter, in which Holmes, after a moment's puzzlement, joined me.

" Thank you. I feel bound to warn you, though, that we risk arrest and possible conviction should we be apprehended by the law, as we will be equipped for house-breaking. Also, as I have mentioned previously, if for some reason our assumptions should prove to be incorrect, we are at risk of suffering the attentions of any members of the gang who may chance to disturb us."

" I am almost of the impression that you do not wish me to come with you," I said.

" Nothing could be further from my mind, I assure you. But I would be remiss if I failed to remind you of the possible risks involved here."

" Have no fear," I confirmed. " I am with you."

" Very good. I expected no less."

I picked up the newspaper, having had no time to read it earlier, and perused a few pages before uttering a cry. " Holmes ! The man Ripley whom we spoke to in Hampstead ! "

" What of him ? "

" He is dead."

" Show me," he ordered, fairly snatching the paper from my hands. He scanned the page. " Found dead in Finsbury Park. Skull crushed by a blunt object. Watch and wallet missing. Pockets emptied. ' Clear case of robbery,' says Lestrade. Ha ! It is nothing of the kind, clearly."

" What do you believe it to be, then ? "

" We know that he was expecting Sir Godfrey, whom I am now convinced has been something less than straightforward in his dealings with us. Somehow, Sir Godfrey is connected with all of this."

" I fail to see how."

" I have my suspicions, but they are as yet unproven. May I suggest that you take a little rest ? You appear to need it."

" And you ? "

" For myself, I can confidently say that the thrill of the chase is sufficient fuel to keep my engine turning. When this is over, I can afford to relax a little, but until this time, it is impossible for me to consider letting down my guard."

I followed Holmes' advice, and lay down in my bedroom for a while, being woken a few hours later by Holmes standing at the foot of the bed. " We will be off in a short while," he said to me. " It is now dark, and a merciful fog has descended, which should ensure that we will remain undetected at our work. Let us eat before we set off. Mrs. Hudson has prepared what promises to be an excellent repast to send us on our way. I have the dark lanterns and the necessary tools all ready."

A little later we set off for Finsbury, and made our way to the back of the house, following the riverside route that de Vries had taken the previous evening. We met no-one on our way, and as Holmes had predicted, the fog hid us from view.

On arrival at the house, Holmes removed a cloth roll from his inside pocket, and proceeded to pick the lock of the back door of the house.

" I had considered jemmying the door, or breaking a window, to simulate the work of ordinary criminals," said he, " but I considered it best if we left as few traces of our entry as possible. It would seem foolish to advertise the fact of our arrival."

On entering the back room, where the large table was in the position where we had first seen it, Holmes checked that the blinds and curtains covering the window were closed before lighting the first of the dark-lanterns.

" Since the whole business must be set up and taken down many times, and accomplished in a short space of time, I am confident that any hiding place will be in this room," he explained.

" Where should we look ? "

" The panels on the wall that forms the division between this room and the space under the staircase will almost certainly provide one hiding-place," he answered, moving to the area of the room he had indicated, and tapping

the walls gingerly with his knuckles. " Ah ! " He grasped
at the side of one of the panels and applied himself to it.
After an initial resistance, the panel suddenly slid to one
side, revealing a cavity into which Holmes shone the lantern. " Chairs," he reported, " and champagne glasses, together with some crates of champagne." He explored the
recess a little further. " No sign of any gaming apparatus,
though," he said.

" If it were cards or dice that formed the components of
the games of chance, they could easily be carried in a pocket, and brought here as needed," I pointed out.

" That is very true, but the gamblers that we have observed are women, and roulette is the game of choice for
most female gamesters. Here, take this," he commanded
me, passing me the other lantern, " and see if you can discover any loose floorboards or concealed trapdoor or anything of that nature. I have a strong suspicion that there
may be a more secret cache beneath our feet."

I followed his example, and dropped to my knees to examine the floor. After a relatively short time I was able to
announce some success. " There is a crack between the
two floorboards here," I informed Holmes, " but I am unsure how to make use of it."

He came to my side, and studied the floor carefully. " I
believe that this is the hiding place we have been seeking, but I confess that I am a little puzzled by its operation." He inserted a thin plasterer's trowel that formed
part of his housebreaker's tools into the crack and moved
it around. " The hinges are here and here," he told me,
pointing to two locations, " which implies that we should
be able to lift the trapdoor from here," plunging the trowel into a crack in the floor at some distance from the first.

After a little struggle, that portion of the floor lifted on hinges, as Holmes had foretold.

" Well, Watson, here we are," he said, gazing down into the shallow hole thus revealed. A roulette wheel and a folded piece of green baize, on which it was possible to discern the markings of a roulette table, were revealed. A small wooden box beside the cloth proved to contain gambling chips, similar to the one that we had discovered earlier. " This is what we came to seek," he said, lifting out the roulette wheel.

He sat on his haunches for some time, examining the wheel, from time to time picking it up and examining the underside before spinning it, sometimes with the ball and sometimes without.

" I think I have it now, Watson," he told me. " Pray, select a number between one and thirty-six."

" Twenty-four," I told him.

" Very good. And I choose seventeen." He spun the wheel and threw the ball into the dish, where it rocketed back and forth until the wheel slowed and stopped, and the ball came to rest in the slot against which stood the number " 17". " Ha ! " he exclaimed. " Again ? "

" Very well," I said, more than a little astounded by this. " I now choose seventeen."

" And I choose thirty-five." He repeated the action of the croupier, and this time also, his prediction was proved correct as the ball entered and stayed in the " 35" slot. " One more time ? "

" Twelve," I said, by now totally bewildered.

" Let me also choose twelve," he said. Not altogether to my surprise, though to my continued confusion, the ball selected " 12" as its resting place.

" Explain," I demanded.

For answer, he turned the wheel upside down and showed me a small iron disk attached to the underside. " A powerful magnet," he explained, and turned the wheel over once more. " Now observe this," he told me, showing the cross-shaped handle used by the croupier to spin the wheel. He spun the handle, and the wheel moved accordingly. " But now," and he pressed down on the handle, now turning it independently of the wheel. " Do you mark this ? One of the arms of the cross is marked with a small dot. When I move the handle in this way, I am moving another magnet inside the wheel which will be attracted to the magnet on the underside. The dot on the handle indicates the position of the magnet. Therefore, if I wish the ball to land on " 12", I point the dot at that slot. In this way, the flow of the game can be controlled, allowing a gambler to win enough to retain his—or in this case, her—interest and keep him or her at the table for long enough to lose money over the long term."

" How did you know what to look for ? " I asked.

" It is my business to know of such things, though I had never seen an actual example before now."

As we spoke, to my horror, I heard the sound of the back door, by which we had entered the house, being opened. I froze, as did Holmes.

" If it is the police, say nothing," Holmes advised me. " Allow me to explain matters."

" And if it is not ? "

" It may be only a tramp seeking shelter for the night. But then again, it may not. You are armed ? "

I shook my head. " My revolver is back at Baker-street. It was my feeling that were we to be apprehended by the police, it would have gone ill enough with us, given that you were carrying tools to be used for breaking and entering.

It struck me that my being armed with a revolver in addition to your equipping yourself as a housebreaker would hardly make the police well-disposed towards us."

Holmes shrugged. " I, too, am unarmed."

By now, the footsteps had reached the door of the room, and a dark figure filled the doorway.

" Mr. Holmes, I presume ? " came a deep voice with a trace of a foreign accent.

" You have the advantage of me," replied Holmes calmly. " May I ask how you became aware of my presence ? "

" De Vries told us you had followed him to the *Friesland* the other night, and told us to expect you here tonight."

I was astounded by this speech, but Holmes merely threw back his head and laughed heartily.

' " Mr. de Vries is obviously a man of talent and perception."

" You've got that right," came another, gruffer, voice from behind the first speaker. Another shape appeared, that of a squat, somewhat bow-legged man, who could be seen to be carrying what appeared to be a club or cosh of some kind in his right hand. " De Vries is a d____ sight cleverer than you have ever been, Mr. Holmes. And there's not going to be much time for you to change that situation, because you and Doctor Watson there are going to stay in this house for a little time—until you ship on board the *Friesland*."

" And then ? " asked Holmes mildly.

" Then you go to feed the fishes in the North Sea." The speaker advanced, and I beheld a bestial face, crowned with a shock of dark hair. He gripped the bludgeon firmly in an attitude that spoke of menace, and I had little doubt that this was the weapon that had been responsible for the death of Ripley, the journalist. " Now if you'll just turn round and face the wall and put your hands behind your back, Mr. Holmes, and you too, Doctor."

I felt that I had little choice but to obey, and Holmes likewise followed suit a second or two later. Out of the corner of my eye, I could see the first man approach Holmes, a length of cord looped around his hands. Acting, I must assume, by sense and sound, since his face was to the wall, Holmes suddenly turned, lashing out at the man with the rope, and receiving for his pains a crack on his head with the bludgeon delivered by the other of our captors, which dropped him like a sack of sand. I instinctively let out a cry, and moved to help him, but received a blow on my own head, and I sank to the ground as everything turned black about me.

When I awoke, I was in the same room as before, sitting on the floor with my hands tied behind me. I attempted to move my hands, but discovered that they were tied to something against which my back was leaning. On turning my head—which occasioned some pain—I discovered that Sherlock Holmes and I were sitting back-to-back, our hands and feet tied in such a way as to almost immobilise us. I groaned aloud, and to my relief, heard Holmes' voice in reply.

" I am glad to have company," he said, in that light somewhat mocking tone which I knew betokened an underlying seriousness of manner. " Are you hurt ? "

" My head aches somewhat ? And you ? "

" The same. I have been attempting for some time to rid us of these bonds, but whoever tied us knows his job only too well. Now you are awake, if you can stand, and I along with you, it may be possible to free ourselves. With some difficulty, and not a little pain on my side, we managed to struggle to our feet, but after some ten minutes' manipulation, even Holmes was forced to admit that there was little or no chance of escaping from the ropes, either those securing our hands or those fastening our feet.

" I am sorry," he sighed, as we sank to the floor. " Sorry to have brought you into this. I must ask your pardon."

" Freely given," I answered him. " You warned me in advance that this could prove hazardous, and I accepted the danger without reservation."

" Then I am at least a little relieved," he said to me. " It is one thing to put oneself in danger, but quite another to expose one's friends to unacceptable risks without their knowledge or their consent."

The matter appeared to be troubling him, and I ascribed his concern at least in part to the blow to the head that I had seen him receive. I endeavoured to reassure him as to my condition and my feelings, but I had little way of knowing if my words had had any effect.

" I am devilish thirsty," he said to me at one point. " I hope they do not intend to let us die of hunger and thirst."

It was hard to know what reply to make to this observation, and I made none. The dawn appeared to be breaking, as a little light was now coming through the narrow gaps in the curtain covering the window, leading me to believe that we had been unconscious for a few hours. The silence became oppressive, and was not relieved by Holmes' humming of a monotonous little ditty that he repeated time and again, but I had not the heart to request him to cease.

Without warning, the door was flung open, and the man whom Holmes had attempted to attack entered the room. " Both awake now, are you ? On your feet, then."

" You could untie us first," I suggested, but this was met with a stony glare.

" On your feet," he repeated, and with difficulty,

Holmes and I struggled to our feet, still roped together, back-to-back.

" This way," snarled our captor, pointing to the door. With difficulty, Holmes and I managed to evolve a method of moving our bound feet together which involved shuffling sideways. It was a painfully slow process, and we were ordered to make our way past the back of the house along the path running beside the river. Once or twice I stumbled, but Holmes' quick reactions kept us from falling, and we eventually reached the road where the carriage we had seen previously was waiting. We were ordered summarily into the carriage, but found it impossible, roped as we were, to enter without assistance, which was grudgingly given. Once we had been pushed inside, the only place for us was on the floor between the seats.

The carriage door was slammed shut, and we were left alone in the interior as the carriage jolted.

" Watson," Holmes said to me in a low tone, and I could perceive the excitement in his voice. " The men who have captured us are fools."

" Why do you say that ? " I answered him, in the same tone.

" Because as we were making our way here, I could feel that my housebreaker's kit was still with me. They have overlooked it, for whatever reason I cannot say. I was not aware of its presence while we were in the room back there just then, but when we stumbled for the second time, I could feel it in my left-hand pocket. It is impossible for me to reach it, but I think it should be possible for you to do so."

By dint of following Holmes' instructions, I could manoeuvre myself into a position where I was able to extract the roll of tools from his pocket. The rocking of the carriage as we travelled made it difficult for me to retrieve it, but at length it lay on the floor between our backs, and I could sense Holmes' hands picking at it and extracting a small blade. In a matter of a few minutes, the pressure on my wrists was relaxed, and I was able to massage my aching wrists in front of my face. Holmes' hands were likewise freed, I saw, and he turned and smiled at me.

" We must give the impression that we are still bound," he told me. " The bonds on our ankles must be untied, and then retied with a knot I will use that will make us appear to be captive, but will allow us to free our legs with a little extra pressure. Untie your ropes now. Do not cut them."

It was a few minutes before Holmes had the ropes on our legs adjusted as he wanted them. " Keep your hands out of sight behind your back," he told me, " as if we were still captive. But before you do that, take this, and slip it inside your coat." He passed me a heavy metal jemmy. " You may find this useful. Now, let us assume the position which our captors expect."

In the event, it was not long before the carriage drew to a stop, and we were roughly assisted out of the carriage. I guessed from the sounds and smells that we were in the area of the docks, and this was confirmed when we shuffled along in our crab-like gait towards the gangplank of a ship that could only be the *Friesland*. I heard the sound of Dutch voices as we made our painful way up the gangplank.

" When I give the word, break your leg bonds in the fashion in which I instructed you, and use that jemmy in the best way that occurs to you," Holmes hissed at me as we reached the deck.

Waiting for us on board was a tall figure wearing a

sailor's pea-coat and a sailor's cap, whom I recognised by
his full beard as de Vries.

" Well, Mr. Holmes," he greeted my friend, in an voice
that betrayed hardly any trace of a foreign accent. " So
glad you could visit me here. And Doctor Watson, too.
You are equally welcome, of course. I regret the fact that
your sojourn with us will be necessarily brief, and you will
be unable to complete the crossing to Rotterdam. But no
matter."

During this mocking speech, I had observed Holmes'
eyes seeking around us. " Now, Watson ! " he cried, and
moved quickly to free his feet from the bonds that wrapped
them, darting to seize a boathook attached to the end of a
long pole, and using it to knock to the deck the taller of
our two guards. For my part, I was a little slower than
Holmes, but was able to rid myself of the ropes, and pulled
the jemmy from its hiding-place inside my coat. It was
with a sense of satisfaction that I turned, my weapon in
my hand, to the other cudgel-wielding brute, who stood,
his mouth hanging stupidly open, seemingly almost unable
to move, rigid with surprise. He raised a feeble hand to attempt to prevent me, but it was with a sense of great satisfaction that I was able to repay, with interest, the blows
that he had inflicted earlier on Holmes and myself, and he
joined his companion on the deck.

I turned to de Vries, but Holmes had anticipated my
move, and had the Dutchman pinned against a bulkhead,
the boathook held horizontally and pressed against the
other's throat.

" You will never get off this boat alive," growled de Vries.

" Oh, I think that will be easy enough to arrange,"
smiled Holmes. " Watson, please do me the favour of examining the contents of our host's right-hand coat pocket.

I advise you to use a little caution in the removal of what you may find there."

The Dutchman thrashed his arms in an attempt to stop my hands from entering the pocket, but Holmes applied a warning pressure to the shaft of the boathook, and the struggles soon ceased. To my surprise, I removed a heavy Enfield revolver, which I hefted, replacing the jemmy in my pocket.

" A British Army pistol ? " I said.

" Hardly surprising," Holmes laughed. " Since you are so familiar with such weapons, Watson, you are best placed to make use of it in such a way as to make Sir Godfrey believe that any attempt to stop us leaving this ship with him as our prisoner will have a very painful result."

" Sir Godfrey ? " I exclaimed in astonishment. " What on earth are you talking about ? "

" See here," said Holmes, releasing his grip on the boathook with one hand, and whipping off the other's cap, to reveal a neatly trimmed, but balding, head of hair. " And here," he added, seizing and tugging at the Dutchman's beard, which, to my complete amazement, came away in his hand, revealing a clean-shaven face that I recognised as that of Sir Godfrey Leighbury ! " A very pleasant little run on your part, Sir Godfrey," said Holmes, " but one which has come to an end, I think."

" Hardly that," replied the other, as I suddenly felt the burly arm of one of the *Friesland*'s sailors encircle my neck and squeeze hard, causing me to drop the pistol. Holmes, I saw, was in a similar plight, with another of the sailors restraining him. We were unable to make any move as Sir Godfrey leaned forward and retrieved the gun. " Mine, I believe," he remarked cheerfully, pocketing the weapon once more. " It is a little cold on deck," he went on.

" Maybe you would be more comfortable in my cabin ? "
He gave an order in Dutch, and Holmes and I were igno-
miniously frogmarched to a small cabin in the superstruc-
ture of the steamship.

Sir Godfrey sat himself behind a desk in the cabin, and
placed the revolver meaningfully in front of him. " I will
order these two," jerking his head towards our two giant
captors, " to leave this cabin and wait by the door. They
will, however, be quick to enter once they hear the sound of
this pistol, which I will fire at you should you attempt to
attack or get the better of me. In the case of either of these
events occurring, you may be certain that your next words
will be your last. Do you understand ? "

Holmes and I grudgingly showed our understanding and
he spoke once again in Dutch, leaving the three of us alone
in the cabin.

" I had sooner that you had not penetrated my disguise
in front of the men. Still, what's done is done, and I am
sure you felt you were acting for the best. So," and here he
leaned forward, and smiled unpleasantly, " what may I tell
you ? Or maybe it would be better if you were to inform
me of what you know, since it will be the last chance that
you will have to show off your much-praised powers."

" I know that you and your wife are behind the scheme
to remove works of art from this country to the Netherlands, using these works of art to pay gambling debts
incurred at an illegal gaming-house operated by you," answered Holmes.

" Correct as far as it goes," acknowledged Sir Godfrey.

" I also believe that this is not a child of your own brain,
but was proposed to you by a certain Mynheer Besselink
when you were posted to the Embassy at The Hague."

The effect on the other was extraordinary. He started

forward in his chair, and gripped the edge of the desk, his knuckles turning white. " How do you know of Besselink and his link to me ? " he cried. " I was under the impression that his name was unknown outside certain restricted circles."

" My dear Sir Godfrey, it is my job to know what others would sooner keep hidden. The name of Jan Besselink has been known to me for some years as one of the foremost dealers in stolen artworks operating in the whole of Europe. I am reasonably certain that he advanced you funds that you had lost while gambling somewhere, and you were unable to pay, for whatever reason. He therefore suggested to you that you open your own gaming-house on your return to London, and pay back your debts with the money you took from your—shall I call them clients ? Your wife was to act as a buttoner."

" I do not understand the term, Holmes," I said.

" In the language of the underworld, a person who pretends to be a gambler, but is actually in the employ of the person or persons organising the gambling, encouraging others to lay down their money, is often referred to as a ' buttoner'. It would seem to me that Lady Celia played that part to perfection, encouraging her friends to visit the house in Finsbury, where they would invariably lose their money, and be forced to part with the family heirlooms in order to settle their debts. This followed from the substitution and sale of the van Dyck painting and of the diamonds in the brooch."

" You have some of it, Holmes, but by no means all," laughed Sir Godfrey. " Though I have to admit that you have been most smart in your deductions, there are one or two details where I think you can stand some correction."

" I shall be happy to hear them," commented Holmes pleasantly.

" First, you should know that your being here is the ultimate result of my plans, rather than of your abilities. I was well aware of the fact that you had discovered the Finsbury house, and that you were following my trail and activities in my guise as de Vries. It was inevitable that these operations would be eventually disclosed to the police, and the business would be shut down, even if I and Celia escaped arrest. Much as I may admire the Dutch and many of their ways, I have no wish to remove myself from England and live surrounded by a flat marsh for the rest of my days. Believe me, your reputation and what I have seen of your meddling methods, of which more anon, left me in no doubt whatsoever of the fact that sooner or later the police would be on my tail."

" I am most gratified to hear your last words. And your response to my ' meddling', as you put it ? "

" As I said, it was to ensure that you and the Doctor here never again troubled my business. But maybe you will understand better if I explain from the beginning how this whole affair began.

" I have always been fond of gaming. Cards, dice, and indeed any game of chance have been an attraction for me from an early age. I married late, after having met my prospective wife in a casino at Monte Carlo. As you may guess from the way that we met, we shared similar tastes, and I found her to be an attractive and intelligent companion. Shortly after our marriage, I was posted to the Hague, as you are aware. As you rightly surmised, I fell into debt there as the result of my gambling, chiefly in the casinos in Belgium which I visited regularly, and I was at my wit's end. Though I was not a poor man, it was impossible for

me to lay my hands on the money that I owed without raising suspicion. The man Besselink first threatened me and
Celia with physical harm, but I was easily able to convince
him that this was no way in which to recover the money I
owed to him.

He therefore suggested, in a fashion which left me no
alternative other than acceptance, the means of repay-
ment that you have described. I was to take, under another name, a London house which would remain ostensibly
empty. However, late at night the house would take on
a new function, that of a gaming-house. I was informed
that you had discovered the gaming apparatus—the roulette wheel, and so forth." Holmes nodded his agreement.
" This was supplied to me by Besselink, with full instructions on how to operate it. I invariably acted as croupier on
the occasions when the casino was open, in my character as
de Vries. At the times when I was supposedly away from
London, as you have probably surmised, I was wearing the
beard and acting the part of a Dutchman. I chose to operate under an alias for a number of reasons, not the least because I am a tolerably well-known figure about Town, and
it would place me at risk were I to be discovered, or even
suspected of, operating such an establishment. The Dutch
personality was one I found easy to adopt. My wife, as you
have divined, brought her friends to gamble and she herself
played at the tables, and appeared to win with sufficient
frequency to encourage her guests.

" Supposedly in order to protect the reputation of the
clients, but in reality to prevent me from being recognised,
it was a rule of the house was imposed requiring everyone, including those staffing the establishment, to wear a
mask. It was amusing, I confess," and here he laughed unpleasantly, " to view the friends of my wife, whom I knew

socially, wager a small fortune on the turn of the wheel that I was controlling and lose it all.

" These times when the house was in operation coincided with the visits of the *Friesland* to London. It was impossible to trust any Englishman with the operations of the gaming house, since it is possible that they would recognise me, even in my disguise as de Vries. All my assistants, the waiters who served the champagne and so on, as well as the coachman who collected the customers and brought them to the house, were Dutch, and came and went on the *Friesland*. In that way, I was the only party involved who remained in England for any length of time, should the police, or some interfering investigator such as you, become interested in the affair."

" I can imagine," Holmes commented drily, " that it was also the case that Besselink wished to keep watch over his investment, if I may term it such, which is why he sent his own men rather than relying on you to provide the help from local sources."

" I fear that you may be correct there. I was constantly reminded—indeed, I still am—that my continued prosperity, such as it is, is the result of Besselink's tolerance." He shuddered, and his voice dropped. " Indeed, I still cannot truly say that I am my own man, even though the original amount that I had owed has been repaid many times over."

" That is often the way with men such as Besselink. One may never break free of the chains that bind them, however hard one tries." Holmes gave an enigmatic smile at this, but I was at a loss to understand his meaning.

" An epigram that applies equally to you at the moment, Holmes," replied the other. " You may somehow have escaped the ropes that bound you, but you are as much in my power as if you were still tied hand and foot."

Holmes shrugged. " As you will. And at what point did the works of art enter the picture, if I may put it that way ? " he asked.

" I think you have already determined that for yourself, have you not ? Naturally, there was nothing so vulgar as cash changing hands within the Finsbury Park house. Instead, each of the gamblers had an open line of credit, of which they invariably took full advantage. It was my task, in my character of de Vries, to make appointments with these ladies at regular intervals and either to collect the money that they owed, or else to deliver the money that was owed to them—though the latter hardly ever took place in practice, as you may imagine. Of course, all such dealings had to be carried out in the form of cash—if they were transacted as bank drafts or any other form of transfer, the gamblers' secret activities would instantly become apparent."

" And naturally," Holmes broke in, " it was impossible for them to lay their hands on such large sums of cash as I presume we are discussing, and accordingly you suggested that the family treasure should be given to you in lieu of cash, and substituted with a forgery ? "

" You have it exactly."

" Including, naturally, the diamonds and the van Dyck painting that you yourself have sent to Holland."

To my amazement, and that of Holmes, Sir Godfrey threw back his head and laughed heartily. " Fear not. They are still in this country," he told us.

Holmes appeared to be astounded. " I can swear that the painting that you gave me to examine was a modern reproduction and that the diamonds in the brooch were not genuine stones."

" You are perfectly correct in those assumptions."

" Then how— ? " Sherlock Holmes appeared perplexed by Sir Godfrey's words.

" They were by way of being something of a test of your abilities. Thanks to Dr. Watson here, your reputation has gone before you, and I could be reasonably certain that one of my victims would employ your services at some time in the future. I confess that I was sceptical as regards your abilities, but even so I determined to set you a little test, or to be more accurate, two little tests—the painting and the brooch. I arranged for a substitute van Dyck to be created—"

" —by the man Visser," broke in Holmes.

" Yes, that was the name he went by when he was in this country. I suppose I may congratulate you on your perspicacity. In any event, you passed the tests with flying colours, and thereby sealed your doom. From the time that you determined the false provenance of the van Dyck, and questioned my servants regarding it—oh yes, I was well aware of your activities in that area—I knew it would only be a matter of time before you discovered the Finsbury house and de Vries, and quite possibly even the *Friesland* and her involvement in the business.

" From then on, it was a matter of leading you into the trap prepared for you. The little dance that I led you round London, Doctor, and all the other little parts of the comedy we played in Finsbury, were all designed ultimately to lead you here."

To say that I was stunned by this information would be an understatement. I had had no idea that we had been walking around London, supposedly on the track of this villain, but in reality, dancing to his tune. Holmes, on the other hand, seemed as unconcerned as if the conversation we were holding was merely concerned with the weather.

" And what happens next ? " he asked our captor.

" Why, I go to Rotterdam, of course. We are already on our way, as you have no doubt observed."

I confess that I had not been conscious of the fact that the *Friesland* had now left the dock, but now that it had been mentioned, I looked out of the cabin window to discover that we were now travelling down the Thames towards the North Sea.

" So you see, Holmes, that there really is nothing you can do," said Leighbury. " As soon as we are out of sight of land, I will give orders for you and the Doctor here to leave the ship over the rail. You will be given every assistance to leave." He regarded Holmes and myself with a singularly unpleasant smile.

" You are making a mistake," Holmes told him in a level tone.

" That being ? "

" You are assuming that you will be in a position to give orders that will be obeyed."

" Have you any reason to believe otherwise ? "

" Most assuredly." Without warning, Holmes lunged for the revolver on the desk, but was unable to prevent Leighbury's hand from closing on it first. However, Holmes' powerful grip prevented the baronet from raising the weapon, much less using it, and the two men strained against each other's strength as Sir Godfrey called loudly for assistance. " Pieter ! Jan ! "

The two Dutchmen who had escorted us to the cabin burst through the door, and Holmes instantly released his grip on Sir Godfrey's wrist, causing it to fly up in the air, still holding the revolver, and involuntarily to pull the trigger, sending a shot through the ceiling. The sudden report caused all in the room to freeze, save for Holmes, who turned towards the two seamen with a friendly smile.

" Do you speak English ? " he asked them.

One shook his head, but the other replied, " A little."

" Please fetch the captain of this ship."

" You are in no position to demand anything," objected Sir Godfrey.

" I am requesting, not demanding," Holmes corrected him. He turned back to the sailor. " I believe that Mynheer Besselink will be interested in what I have to tell your captain."

At the mention of Besselink, the sailor's formerly wooden countenance changed. " Very good. No tricks," he warned Holmes as he left the cabin.

" There will be none. I give you my word," Holmes assured him.

The four of us, Sir Godfrey, the Dutch sailor, Holmes, and myself, stood in an awkward silence until the seaman returned with the ship's captain, a stocky Dutchman, with a pipe in the corner of his mouth.

" Well ? " said the latter to Holmes in excellent English. " The famous Sherlock Holmes. Under most circumstances, I would be pleased to see you. Under the current circumstances, my feelings are mixed. You have business with me, I believe ? "

" Indeed I do. Pray, have the goodness to feel inside my coat here, and retrieve the paper you find there. I would do it myself, but I fear that a movement of that type might well disturb Sir Godfrey, and cause him to let off that pistol with which he is playing."

The captain looked at Holmes strangely, but followed Holmes' request, removing an envelope, opening it, and studying the paper inside. He glanced from the paper to

Sir Godfrey's face, and then back again, an expression of concern growing on his own countenance.

" What the devil is that paper, Holmes ? " enquired the baronet.

" It is, as the captain is discovering, a full statement of your accounts, including the money paid in by a Mynheer de Vries to the account of Sir Godfrey Leighbury. Money, the existence of which, I believe, was never communicated to Besselink."

" Where did you lay hold of that paper, in God's name ? "

" My friend Sir David Abrahams was of great assistance to me."

" The banker ? "

" The same. He and I have an acquaintance, and I thought it provident to discover some of the facts of the matter through him."

" You d____ blackguard ! " barked Sir Godfrey, raising the revolver, and aiming it at Holmes. A quick command from the captain, and the baronet's arm was seized and twisted behind his back by one of the sailors, causing the baronet to utter a cry of pain, and drop the gun.

" That is nearly fifteen thousand pounds you have stolen from us," the captain accused Leighbury.

" I computed the total at fourteen thousand, eight hundred and seventy-two pounds, twelve shillings and eleven pence," remarked Holmes pleasantly.

" Thank you," answered the captain, with a thin smile. He turned to Sir Godfrey. " That money will be repaid to us as soon as we return to London."

" That will not be possible," mumbled the baronet.

" Why not ? "

The other looked at the floor, and uttered in a voice so

low that I had to strain my ears to make out the words, " I
have lost it all at Newmarket."

" *U stomme dwaas* ! You stupid fool ! Now I see your
losses listed at the bottom here," and he waved the paper before him. He regarded Sir Godfrey with a look of
contempt. " You will continue your journey with us, as
planned," he informed him. " Whether you will reach Rotterdam or not, I have yet to make up my mind." The other
blanched at his words.

" You cannot do this ! " he protested.

" I can if I so desire. I am master of this ship, and my
word is law here. I believe that Mynheer Besselink will
have no objection to the removal of a traitor."

" But my wife ! " fairly wailed the other. " What is to
become of Celia ? "

" That is a question you should have asked yourself
before commencing your treachery." The captain faced
Holmes and myself. " And now I am faced with the question of what to do with you two."

" May I be permitted to make a suggestion ? " asked
Holmes in a courteous tone. The other nodded. " Since
it is clear that Sir Godfrey is no longer to be trusted to
run the operation, which has now obviously run its course,
there would seem to be little point in disposing of Dr.
Watson and myself in the manner originally proposed by
Sir Godfrey, other than that of pure revenge. You do not
strike me as being the kind of man to indulge himself in
that way, captain."

" There is some logic in what you say," replied the
Dutchman.

" Therefore, I propose that you provide us with a boat
for us to make our own way to land. Sir Godfrey we will
leave to your sense of justice. Naturally, when we reach the

coast, I will inform the authorities that the *Friesland* is to be watched, and should she endeavour to enter a British port in the future, her crew will be subject to arrest and detention."

" And my wife ? Celia ? " repeated the hapless baronet, who now seemed to have lost all his spirit.

" We will inform her of what has occurred, and she can arrange things as she sees fit," Holmes answered him.

The captain bowed slightly to Holmes. " I agree. As you say, this race is won, and we cannot take it further. The roulette wheel and all the associated apparatus are on board here, and will never be seen again in England. In any event," he smiled, " it will be a relief for me not to have to endure your English beer again. I have no objection to bidding a final farewell to your country in that regard, at least."

" May I enquire of the fate of the artworks that were delivered to you and have made their way across the sea ? "

" That I do not know," replied the captain. " They are delivered to Besselink, and after that, they become his affair, not mine. Come, let us to the boat. You and the Doctor can row a few miles ? Jan, Pieter." He gave an order in Dutch that I took to be orders to guard Sir Godfrey.

Once out of the cabin, the captain turned to Holmes. " I could not say it in front of that man or my seamen, but it would have gone against my nature to throw you and the Doctor into the sea. It is my pleasure to be able to assist you." So saying, he had one of the ship's boats prepared for us, and provided us with water and some food, as well as a map and compass. " You are here," he said, pointing to the chart. " The tide is on the ebb, so I would recommend this course, and you should make land somewhere near here," with his finger on the town of Gravesend. " That is, of course, if you are not fortunate enough to be spotted and picked up by another ship."

The boat was swung overboard, and the captain sent a seaman down the ladder, both to help us into the boat, and to point out the workings of our small craft before ascending again and casting us adrift.

Holmes and I spelled each other at the oars on our tedious journey towards land. It was a matter of some hours before we reached land—a mudbank some two miles from Gravesend, as the tide had carried us in an unintended direction, and both Holmes and I were fatigued by the events of the previous hours, followed by the hard manual labour at the oars. Indeed, Holmes seemed to be in a condition where it was necessary for me to assist him on the road towards the town. We had refreshed ourselves a little with the water and the bread and Gouda cheese that the Dutch captain had provided for us, but I felt in need of greater sustenance, and it was with relief that I espied the sign of a wayside inn.

On entering the saloon bar, however, we were unceremoniously ejected, and ordered in no uncertain terms to take ourselves to the public bar. Once there, I caught sight of myself in the mirror behind the bar, and forced myself to look at Holmes with as dispassionate an eye as I could manage. I had to admit that neither of us presented an attractive sight. After lying on the floor of the Finsbury house, our journey on the floor of the carriage, and our subsequent adventures, including a tramp through the mudflats, we presented an appearance of which many tramps would have been ashamed.

Happily, a few shillings remained in my pockets after all the recent events, and I was able to order two glasses of ale, a pork pie, together with some bread and good

English cheese, which we took to the corner of the bar and devoured hungrily, restoring our strength a little.

" And now ? " I asked Holmes.

" We return to town and we confront Lady Celia."

" When we appear like this ? " I asked, looking down at my appearance.

" Indeed. I think it will lend greater force to our story. Come," finishing his beer, " to the station. I take it you have no objection to travelling third-class ? "

" I think that in this state we have little choice," I laughed.

On our arrival at London Bridge station, it was hard for us to persuade a hansom to carry us to Amberfield House, but by dint of showing all the silver in our pockets, we were able to convince a cabbie that we were not as destitute as our appearance would suggest, and that he would receive due compensation for his labour.

On arrival at our destination, we rang the front door-bell, whereupon the butler who opened the door took one glance at us before attempting to shut the door in our faces. Holmes had foreseen this move, however, and planted his foot firmly between door and jamb, and presented a card to the butler.

" I think you will find that if you give that card to Lady Celia, she will be anxious to see me, regardless of the current state of my person."

" Very good, sir," replied the stolid servant. " Please wait outside while I consult her Ladyship." He returned very shortly, breathing hard and his face red. " Her Ladyship will see you and your friend, Mr. Holmes. This way, please."

Unhappily conscious of my dishevelled and muddy

appearance, I allowed myself to be led across the hallway
to the drawing-room where we were greeted by Lady Celia.

" Where is Godfrey ? " were her first words to us, as soon
as the door had closed behind the butler, even before any
words of greeting.

" By my estimation, he is somewhere between here and
Rotterdam. But whether he is currently on the surface of
the North Sea, or under it, I have no way of telling."

Her hands flew to her mouth, and she uttered a convul-
sive sob. " Why are you still alive ? " she demanded fu-
riously of Holmes. " It is you who is meant to be at the
bottom of the ocean ! " So saying, she flew against him,
and dashed her fists against his body. Holmes grasped her
wrists with a grip of iron, and held her fast while he stared
down at her.

" Your husband has done a very foolish thing," Holmes
told her. " Not only has he broken the law, he has been
cheating an extremely dangerous man, and is now facing
the consequences." He detailed the events of the day, and
concluded with, " I came here to—"

" —to arrest me, I know. Do your worst, Mr. Sherlock
Holmes. I am not frightened of the law."

" No, I came here to tell you that you also are in danger.
Men such as Jan Besselink are vindictive, and will seek
their revenge, not just on those whom they consider have
done them wrong, but on those close to them."

" What should I do ? "

" You have two choices. You may either choose to leave
this country and fly to another continent, where you will
live the life of a fugitive for the rest of your days, never
knowing whether the next man you meet in the street may
be your assassin. It would be a life of fear until you die."

Lady Celia gazed up with tears in her eyes. " You do not make it sound appealing," she said.

" It is not appealing," he answered her. " The alternative is to throw yourself on the mercy of the justice system of this country. You may well be safer inside prison than outside it. And who knows, by the time you are released, Besselink will, I trust, be in no position to harm others."

" There is a third way," cried the wretched woman. " Besselink may attempt to kill me, but I am able to forestall him ! "

" I do not think you possess the courage for that course of action," replied Sherlock Holmes. " Oh, you might persuade others that you had attempted to make away with yourself, but you know, and I know too, that you would never be able to follow through with it."

" So you are telling me that I should give myself up to the police ? "

" I feel it would be your safest move under the circumstances."

" I will stay here and take my chances against the law and against Besselink. You have no real evidence against me, save the word of a man who now is probably dead, according to your account."

" The police would have my word and the word of those whom you duped."

" Your word ! " she laughed gaily. " And my friends' word ? They know nothing, save the fact that they lost money at a roulette table, and were forced to sell the family treasures to settle their debts. Do you really think that they will be happy to stand in the witness box and announce that fact, even if they suspected anything underhand ? Believe me, Mr. Holmes, I am not destitute, in any event. I can afford to hire a lawyer who can tear to tiny shreds any case that you or the police may choose to bring against me."

These were palpable hits, and Sherlock Holmes stood there, nonplussed for a short time before recovering himself. " Very well," he said stiffly. " I have given you fair warning of your danger. If you choose to ignore it, that is your affair." With that, he turned on his heel and stalked out of the room, through the front door which the butler sprang to open for him, and into the street, myself following him.

" She is demonstrably and d__ably in the right, Watson," he complained to me, as we walked back to Baker-street. There is no way that any charges could be successfully brought against her. I fear, though, that she fails to appreciate the extreme danger in which she lies."

" I do not see how you could possibly have made the matter any clearer to her," I assured him. " But I am puzzled. How did you come to suspect Sir Godfrey of being de Vries ? "

" I knew it as soon as we first caught sight of de Vries," he answered. " If you remember, I said to you regarding the gamblers at the house that a person's figure and gait were sometimes as distinctive as his or her face, if not more so ? Maybe you remarked that slight inward twist of the left foot when Sir Godfrey walked ? No ? I am surprised, as it was most distinctive, and unique, when coupled with that forward cast of the shoulders. When I observed the figure known as de Vries to exhibit the same characteristics, it became clear to me that de Vries and Sir Godfrey were one and the same person. When you likewise consider that it was only when Sir Godfrey was absent from London that de Vries was active, and *vice versa*, it was clear that the two personages were indeed one and the same man."

" And Lady Celia ? "

" It was inconceivable to me that she could visit such an establishment frequently and regularly and fail to recognise her husband, even masked and disguised. It was clear, therefore, that she was party to the deception, and was almost certainly playing an active role in guiding her friends there."

" Did you suspect that there was a trap set for us ? "

" I feared that might be the case, and accordingly I had prepared my trump card."

" The list of transactions you obtained from Abrahams ? "

" The same. I had trusted to the vanity common to many criminals which would cause our captor to speak. Once he had opened his mouth, he would allow me to open mine, and play my ace."

" Then we were never in any real danger ? "

" On the contrary, my dear fellow, we were in very palpable danger at many times in the past days. I attempted to warn you of it, but like the brave British bulldog that you are, you stuck by me faithfully, for which I am most grateful. I apologise once again most profoundly for having placed you in the situation in which we found ourselves."

" When did you first suspect the trap ? "

" I knew something was amiss when I was handed the brooch. The stones were obviously false, and did not require my expertise to discover the fact. Furthermore, they were clumsily set, leading me to believe that they were temporary, and would be replaced, probably by the real stones, at some time in the near future. At that moment, I knew that whatever was happening was almost certainly of a more complex nature than it first appeared. But it was the link between Sir Godfrey and de Vries that made me certain of the true state of affairs.

Ah, here we are at 221B. I suggest we make our way upstairs quietly, so as not to alarm Mrs. Hudson with our appearance, and after we have made ourselves a little more presentable, and restored our outer appearance, we take care of the inner man with a visit to Alberti's and a spot of dinner ? "

HIS ADVENTURE had an unhappy ending. Some ten days after the events described above, it was reported in the newspaper that Lady Celia Leighbury, the wife of the missing baronet Sir Godfrey Leighbury, had been run down and killed while walking along Regent-street by a carriage whose horses had unaccountably started and bolted, and crushed her under the carriage wheels.

" It was to be expected," said Holmes. " But never fear, I will see Besselink in the dock before long," but it was a promise it nevertheless took him two years to fulfil, with the aid of the police agents of four countries.

SHERLOCK HOLMES AND THE CURIOUS AFFAIR OF THE ARCHDEACON

EDITOR'S NOTE

A story of a very different aspect to other adventures. Written on foolscap sheets, pinned together, with several corrections and crossings-out; this was presumably a foul copy, and one which Watson did not feel it was worth his while continuing, possibly considering it too slight for publication. However, I found this to be a different side to the great detective. Incidentally, this case is mentioned in passing at the beginning of The Red Circle.

The city of Larrowby is mentioned here, but since there is no city in England by that name, it is obvious that Watson was using this as a pseudonym for some other northern city, such as Lincoln or York.

F ALL THE ADVENTURES that I shared with the consulting detective, Mr. Sherlock Holmes, I do not believe that any presented as amusing an aspect as the one I relate here.

It was late November, and the previous night's thick fog still enveloped London on the morning that Mr. Fairdale Hobbs came to visit us with his concerns. A young man of about twenty-five, his rather delicate features and weak chin were somewhat offset by a slightly incongruous bristling moustache, whose sandy colour matched his lank hair, worn slightly long. He had the air of a gentleman, and was dressed in the conventional style of a young man who works in an office, but his garments appeared to be a little out of the current fashion, and had seen better days.

" It may seem trivial to you, Mr. Holmes, but it is a worry to me, and I would be obliged if you would take this case on my behalf," were his first words to us, following his self-introduction.

" I cannot possibly tell you if I will take the case or not," answered my friend, smiling, " until you present me with some of the relevant facts."

" Of course," replied our visitor. " First, maybe I should explain something about myself—"

" Please proceed. Other than the facts that you are a bachelor, you reside in a lodging-house in Great Orme-street, you are employed as a clerk in the City, and though this employment is not generously rewarded, you have oc-casionally received gifts in kind from your relatives who live outside London in the North of the country, I know nothing about you."

The other appeared startled. " How do you know these things about me ? " he demanded, in some consternation.

" The fact that you are a bachelor is, I fear, obvious from the state of your coat, which has not been brushed for some time, and from which a button is hanging by a thread. No wife would permit her husband to be seen in such a state. I deduce Great Orme-street from the leaf of a species of Japanese maple adhering to one shoe. This particular spe-cies of tree is, to the best of my knowledge, only to be found in Russell-square by the side of that street which contains so many lodging-houses, and also in Kew Gardens. Since I do not believe you reside in Kew Gardens..."

" Yes, yes, and the rest ? "

" As to the lodging-house, permit me to say that you have the lean and hungry look of a man who has breakfast-ed, and that not too well, on lodging-house fare. A man who prepares his own breakfast, or who has his breakfast prepared for him by a loving spouse, has a different out-look on the world from one who is forced to subsist on the

matutinal offerings of a London landlady. Always except-
ing our own Mrs. Hudson, of course, do you not agree,
Watson ?

" It is obvious from the style of your hat and your boots
that you are employed in the City, and the crease on your
sleeve, not to mention the peculiar callouses on your hand
developed by those who make their living pushing a pen
across the page, show me the nature of your employment.
The hat is of the finest quality, but I notice the label of
a provincial hatter in the Northern city of Larrowby, and
it is of a style of some two years ago, from which I may
deduce that you were presented it at that time by a relative who lives in that city, since it is not the kind of gift I
would expect to be presented by a mere friend."

" You are correct in every detail," cried the young man.
" And indeed, it is regarding my uncle, Archdeacon James
Harper-Barrington, who has been remarkably generous to
me, that I wish to consult you.

You may be aware that my uncle, my mother's brother, is the Archdeacon in one of our dioceses, indeed that of
Larrowby, the city to which you have just referred. He has
held the post for about fifteen years, and though there was
talk at one time of his being elevated to a bishopric, this
now appears to be unlikely. He has expressed little interest
in such a promotion, but continues his calling, by all accounts efficiently. He is a well-liked figure within the diocese, as far as I can tell, and his generosity has not merely
been confined to me.

" My parents are both deceased, with the Archdeacon
being my closest relative, and I his. Accordingly, I have
fallen into the habit of travelling to Larrowby for my holidays and spending my time with him. Though there is a
considerable difference in our ages, I find the time I spend

with him to be congenial, and I believe the feeling is reciprocated. He and I share an interest in several different matters, one of which is the art and architecture of the
Middle Ages, and we have spent many happy days together exploring the riches of the diocese. Indeed, you may
even have heard of him in connection with the monographs
he has published on the development of the Perpendicular
style of architecture. He is seen by many as the definitive
authority on the subject.

" As you correctly stated, he has been generous towards
me and towards others. Indeed, one might almost say that
he has been too generous."

" On what grounds could that accusation of over-gener-
osity be levelled ? "

" It appears to me that his charitable outgoings are more
than could be explained by his earnings as the Archdeacon,
the amount of which is known to me."

" He has private means ? "

" He is my late mother's brother. The family, although
one of the oldest in England, is by no means wealthy. I am
somewhat at a loss to account for his generosity."

" Perhaps you can give instances ? "

" Despite my rather shabby appearance," and here our
visitor smiled a little shamefacedly, " I never come away
from a visit to my uncle without at least fifty pounds to my
name, and this occurs several times each year."

" A goodly sum," I commented.

" Indeed it is. It represents a significant part of his in-
come as a clergyman. And I may add that he spares no
expense to entertain me when I visit. If that were all, it
would be understandable, but to my certain knowledge he
has given to charitable objects many times the amount he

gives to me. It is incomprehensible to me how he can lay his hands on these sums."

" May I be impertinent," said Holmes, " and enquire how you spend the money that you receive from your uncle ? "

The other flushed slightly. " I present it to worthy causes—societies dedicated to conversion of the heathen, for example—and so on. In my younger days I also felt that I might also take Holy Orders, but I was never fully persuaded of the sincerity of my calling. However, the wish to do good for others has never left me. My salary with Connington's is not excessive, but it is sufficient for my needs. Sometimes, though, my uncle presents me with a gift which is not money—this hat, for example."

" You have worries about your uncle's money ? "

" Indeed. I cannot make out its source."

" And you are concerned that the source may prove to be—how shall I say this ? Not in your uncle's best interests were it to be made public ? "

" You have it in a nutshell, Mr. Holmes."

" Have you any reason to believe this ? "

" I regret to say that I have. I have recently returned from a visit to my uncle, and it was what I saw there that has in part prompted my visit to you. The other portion I will relate in due course and occurred only yesterday evening.

" While I was last staying at my uncle's house, he was, as always, the very soul of hospitality. He entertained me splendidly, and he and I visited many old parish churches in the region, and in the evenings worked together on the preparation of his forthcoming volume on the carvings to be found on some of the west doorways.

" One morning, I came downstairs before my uncle. We

had been working late the previous evening on the book I have just mentioned, and to my mind, there were several questions that remained unanswered which I wished to verify. It may sound trivial to you, Mr. Holmes, but I had actually lain awake in the night, concerned as to which of two medieval masons might have been responsible for the carving of a group of devils over the door of a church. It was a topic that had vexed my uncle and myself the previous evening, and I had taken myself off to bed, leaving him poring over the subject."

Here Holmes broke in, smiling. " Were you and your uncle at odds over the issue of this unknown mason ? " he enquired.

" By no means. We were unanimous in our puzzlement over the matter. Indeed, we were in one mind on almost everything. In any event, when I arrived downstairs I was astonished. On the desk where we had been working together the previous night was an envelope addressed to a Miss Kitty Bellecharme with a poste restante address at the Larrowby post office. The envelope had been opened, and the contents removed. However, to my surprise, I noted the torn fragments of such a letter in the wastepaper basket in my uncle's study. The paper had been torn into tiny pieces, so that it was impossible to make out more than a few isolated phrases, but there was one scrap a little larger than the rest on which I could read the words, 'need more passion'. All else had been ripped into shreds so small that only half a word at most was visible. There was no way of deciphering any more. As you may imagine, my time was limited, as I expected my uncle to descend for breakfast at any moment."

" Did you notice a postmark on the envelope ? "

" Indeed I did. It was a London postmark, from the SW district."

" What did you make of this ? "

" I have to confess that I had not the faintest glimmering, other than some form of affaire or intrigue. But such a position would be completely out of character for my uncle."

" Maybe it could be intended for one of the servants ? " I suggested.

Our visitor shook his head. " My uncle lives very quietly with only a housekeeper and a cook to serve his needs. Both are elderly, and the idea of passion being attached to either is, quite frankly, more than a little ludicrous, if I may say so."

" The writing on the scrap of paper that you found, and the writing on the envelope. Were they in the same hand ? " asked Holmes.

" It would be very hard to give an answer to that question, given the few words that I saw. I believe that they probably were written by the same person. Now that I come to recollect matters more clearly, they were written with the same pen and ink."

" By a man or by a woman ? "

" I would have to guess that they were written by a woman, but I cannot be certain of that."

" You made no remark to your uncle about the matter ? "

" Naturally, I did not."

" Very well. Pray continue with your narrative. I perceive that you have more to tell us."

" Indeed I do. That very evening, I discovered another event that gave me even more cause to worry. I entered the study, to discover my uncle standing in front of a roaring fire. He turned, with a look of what I would almost have sworn was terror upon his face, the fire blazing at his back. He gazed at me in silence for a good ten seconds or more, I would say, before rushing wordlessly from the room. Immediately I made my way to the fireplace, but all I could see were the charred remains of several sheets of paper in the grate. However one corner had escaped the flames and had fallen onto the fender. Written on it, in my uncle's writing, were the words, 'I will always adore you, with all my heart, and I pray that this passion will never—' and there the words come to an end."

" You say the words ' come to an end' in the present tense. Is it possible that you have saved the scrap of paper ? " Holmes asked eagerly.

" I have it here," withdrawing a stout manila enveloped from his pocket.

" Excellent," commented my friend, taking the envelope, and moving to the window, where he proceeded to extract a small piece of paper, a few inches on a side, and examined it through a lens, holding it up to the light, without, however, passing any opinion on it. After a few minutes, he passed it to me, and returned to his chair. I repeated Holmes' examination, but it appeared that I held an ordinary piece of paper in my hand, with nothing to mark it as being in any way out of the ordinary. The writing was in an old-fashioned round-hand style, splendidly legible, and with, to my eyes, a firm distinction of character visible. I laid the scrap of paper down, and returned to my own seat.

" You are positive that it is your uncle's hand ? " Holmes asked our visitor.

" There is no doubt in my mind as to that fact."

" And the interpretation that you put on these words ? "

" Surely it is obvious, Mr. Holmes ! This can be nothing

other than a copy of a love-letter, a billet-doux, addressed to this Kitty Bellecharme."

" It is of course possible," answered Holmes, " that this Miss Bellecharme is not the intended recipient of this letter, but is a go-between your uncle and the fair correspondent who addresses him from London. It would, after all, be embarrassing for her letters to be delivered directly to his residence, would it not ? "

" That is an alternative that had not occurred to me," confessed the other.

" Did you subsequently mention this incident to your uncle, or he to you ? "

" I did not. Indeed, he seemed to be avoiding my eye, almost for the remainder of my visit. He did, however, present me with his customary largesse on my departure, and though he appeared distant, there was no hint of hostility in his manner."

At this point I interjected my thoughts. " Could it be the case, Mr. Hobbs, that the paper you discovered in the fireplace is not a love letter addressed to a human being ? " I noticed both Hobbs and Holmes regarding me with an air of puzzlement, and hastened to explain, with some embarrassment on my part. " Could this have been the remnants of some devotional work, a sermon, perhaps, expressing your uncle's love of God or some similar sentiment ? "

Holmes gave me a glance of what I flatter myself was some degree of admiration. " An intriguing suggestion, Watson. Well, Mr. Hobbs ? "

" I do not think that would be the case. My uncle's religion is of a rather more down-to-earth, and I might say practical, nature. Such sentiments expressed in a sermon of his, or even in his private writings, would be as much of a surprise to me as the discovery of a love-letter."

" And yet there was the paper with those words. How many sheets of paper would you estimate were burned ? "

" It is almost impossible to say."

" One ? Two ? Many ? " Holmes pressed his enquiry.

Hobbs appeared to be concentrating as he closed his eyes. " Now I come to recall, there was a considerable quantity of paper ashes in the grate. Perhaps one or two quires— that is to say, between twenty-five and fifty sheets."

Holmes made no comment on this, but merely remarked, " Forgive this question, which may seem to be something of a personal one, but do you have any expectations from your uncle ? "

" I believe that my uncle regards me as a son in all but name. He has never married, and since the death of my mother, his sister, I believe myself to be his only relative. Our relations have always been of the most affectionate. We were always close, since I was a boy, but since the death of my parents some years ago, he has taken the place of a father in my life. Indeed, he has said as much to me on more than one occasion, informing me that I was to be his principal legatee. He is not wealthy, but he is not a poor man. I have been led to believe that I would earn some two hundred pounds per annum via the interest on the capital sum that is willed to me. My uncle is without doubt an open and honest man, and I have no reason to disbelieve him in this matter."

" You are on good terms with him, obviously."

" Indeed. As I say, I would regard him almost as a fa- ther, until the curious incident that occurred yesterday."

" Ah, yes, you mentioned that earlier. The details, if you please."

" Imagine my surprise, when I was walking in Piccadil- ly yesterday evening when I believed I saw my uncle on the other side of the road, walking in the opposite direction to me. He was walking slowly, accompanied by a woman, who was completely unknown to me and whose features were obscured by the scarf that she had wrapped around her face. The fog made it difficult for me to be certain of my uncle's identity, but I hailed the man I took to be him, whereupon he looked up, and seeing me, started with an expression of what I took to be recognition, and turned his back on me. As he looked up, I was even more sure that it was he, and that he had recognised me also. I did not feel that it was my place to intrude on his privacy, and so I walked on. After I had walked perhaps fifty yards I turned to look after him, but he and his companion had vanished into the crowds. I confess to having felt slighted by the cut, for which there was no reason that I know of."

" You are certain it was he ? "

" Indeed I am. It could be no other. Besides, as I said, he appeared to recognise me when I called to him."

" And when did you see him last before then ? "

" A matter of some two Sundays ago. We parted on the very best and most affectionate of terms, and we had exchanged letters twice since that time."

" Was he accustomed to visiting London ? "

" Four or five times in the year, I would say. He invariably informed me of his plans, and though I am unable to provide him with lodging at Mrs. Warren's in Great Orme-street, we spend as much time together as our respective businesses will permit."

" Where does he lodge when he is in London ? "

" At his club, the Carlton."

" Do you know if he lodged there last night ? "

" I have not yet discovered that."

" No matter. It is simple for us to confirm the fact.

Obviously you have not attempted to visit him or to make contact since that encounter in Piccadilly. What exactly do you wish me to do for you ? "

" I wish to know what is happening with regard to the mysterious letters and paper that I have discovered, and my uncle's secretive visit to London. For obvious reasons, I do not wish you to let him know that I have retained you. And on that score ..? "

" My fee, I think you will discover, will be well within your ability to pay. Do not fear on that regard. Should, however, I become forced to lay out a little more money than is usual on such occasions, I will inform you."

" Very good. Thank you for your assistance. Please contact me at the address on my card. It may cause some raised eyebrows at Connington's if I am to receive communications from a well-known detective."

" Indeed so, Mr. Hobbs. I hope to have good news for you soon. I will retain this paper that you retrieved, if I may. I hope to discover some use for it."

Our visitor left us, and the door closed behind him.

" Well, Watson ? " Holmes enquired of me, as was his wont on these occasions. I do not believe that he asked me these questions with any great faith in my abilities, but used me more as a sounding-board on which he could expound his theories.

" A pleasant enough young man," I answered. " I see no reason to doubt his story."

" Nor I. Let us see about this uncle. Pass me Crockford's, would you, please ? "

I passed him the clerical directory, and he quickly located the relevant entry. " Yes, as we were told. He seems to be active in a number of charitable activities."

" Blackmail, do you think, Holmes ? An unwise liaison which is threatened with exposure ? "

" I would sooner expect it to be the other way around. That is to say, the Archdeacon being threatened with exposure rather than he being the potential publicist of another's folly. But your notion is by no means without the bounds of possibility."

" But you have no ideas at present ? "

" None that are definite as yet. I think it is time for me to visit the Carlton. Will you accompany me on this little expedition ? "

" Willingly."

" Come, then."

The fog wrapped itself around us as we ventured into the street, and attempted, without success, to hail a hansom to take us to the Carlton. As we walked along the streets, almost deserted, Holmes appeared to be in a brown study.

" I am in two minds, Watson, as to whether to continue with this case," he remarked, as we turned the final corner. " Were it not for the rather outré nature of the events that have been described to us, I would throw it up."

" Surely there is nothing in it that can be described as outré," I objected, " other than the occupation and position of the protagonist."

" Not so," he answered me curtly. " There are several points of interest. Consider, for example, the type of paper—a Dartford foolscap, judging by what remained of the watermark. Hardly the kind of paper one would choose to write an intimate letter, even as a draft. There is also the quantity of paper to be considered. Ah, we are here." We had arrived at the Carlton Club, and Holmes sent in his card, with a request that we wished to see the Venerable Harper-Barrington. After a few minutes, the Club servant to whom we had addressed our enquiry returned with the news that the Archdeacon had left the Club premises shortly after breakfast, and was not expected to return, his luggage having been sent on to King's Cross railway station, from which he would make his way home.

" We appear to be somewhat out of luck," remarked Holmes, as we turned away. As we started along the street, I was engaged in winding my muffler about my face in an attempt to keep the yellow fog from entering my lungs, and so failed to remark the elderly gentleman with whom I came into collision.

" Dear me, I trust that you are not too badly hurt," he exclaimed, in a solicitous tone, the parcel which he was carrying having struck against my ribs.

" Not at all," I assured him. " But I perceive that you have dropped something," I added, noticing some papers lying on the pavement, and stooping to retrieve them. Holmes assisted me to collect the sheets, and I handed them back to their owner, who, I now noticed, was wearing a clerical collar below a cherubic round face, framed by a mane of flowing white hair.

" That is most kind of you," he said to me, as I helped him adjust his coat and scarf, which had been disarranged by the collision. " I was on my way to the Club there, having left there a book which would sadly incommode me by its absence. Maybe I can persuade you, and your friend," glancing at Holmes, " to allow me to procure some refreshment on such an inclement day ? "

At that moment, the Club porter to whom we had spoken earlier caught sight of our little party, and came bustling up to us. " Excuse me, sir," he said to my new companion, " but these two gentlemen was looking for you just now."

He turned to Holmes. " This gentleman here, sir, is the Archdeacon who you was looking for."

" Thank you, Barsett," said the Archdeacon, looking at Holmes with a new interest. " I do not believe we are acquainted, sir."

" My name is Sherlock Holmes," my friend answered him. " Your name was mentioned to me at a meeting of some antiquarian society as an expert in medieval architecture. My informant, whose name unfortunately escapes me at present, told me that you were a member of the Carlton Club here, but was unable to remember your address up North. I came here hoping to discover your address in order to write to you, but it is the most amazing stroke of luck for me to have discovered you here in person."

The old gentleman fairly beamed at this recognition. " Bless my soul ! " he exclaimed. " Why, certainly, had you any specific question in mind that you wished to ask ? Do, do, come inside and take a glass with me. I insist."

Holmes and I followed him into the Club, where we were rapidly provided with glasses of sherry, and Holmes and the Archdeacon were soon engaged in a lengthy and abstruse conversation regarding the development of the decorated capitals of pillars to be found in parish churches of that era. I think I have remarked elsewhere regarding the extraordinary depth of learning that Holmes was able to display in so many areas of knowledge—a depth which would have marked any other man as an expert who had spent his whole life studying the subject. It was so in this instance, where Holmes was perfectly at home with the intricacies of the topic, citing sources and authorities with a fluency that seemed to amaze even our host.

" My dear Mr. Holmes," he exclaimed at one point. " I had flattered myself that I was knowledgeable on these

matters, but your learning appears to exceed mine." Holmes waved a deprecatory hand. " You must surely come and
visit some day. Here is my card. Pray feel free to invite
yourself, and your friend, of course."

" I hardly deserve the compliment," protested Holmes.
" But if you would be kind enough to write for me here the
name and author of the monograph to which you just referred, I would be most grateful."

" Nothing easier," the cleric told him, writing a few
words on a piece of club paper, and handing them over to
my friend. " If you two gentlemen will excuse me, I must
collect the book which I left in my room here, and then
make my way to the station, where I trust I will be reunit-
ed with my luggage, and I will make my way home. A very
good day to you gentlemen, and I am happy to have made
your acquaintance."

As we walked back to Baker-street, Holmes was smiling
softly to himself, wrapped in his own thoughts, on which
I saw no reason to intrude. His first action when we entered our rooms was to take the charred corner of paper
that had been presented to us by Hobbs, and compare it
with the written sheet that had been given to him by the
Archdeacon.

" The writing is indubitably the same, do you not agree ?
More to the point, it would seem that the paper itself is
similar, if not identical."

" What sort of clergyman would write love letters at his
club ? " I asked.

" Your reasoning is false on two points," Holmes corrected me. " Firstly, even if this paper is club notepaper,
which is yet to be proven, that does not mean that it was
used at the club. It may well have been removed and used
elsewhere."

" I grant you that," I answered. " And your second point ? "

" It is possible that this is not a love letter."

" Then what is it ? "

" I believe we will discover when we have made another call. This afternoon is an appropriate time, I would say, following a visit to the concert hall. I do not consider that we are engaged in a matter of life and death here, and I have no other pressing business right now."

" Where do you propose going ? "

" As I was assisting the reverend gentleman to retrieve the papers that had dropped, I remarked an envelope addressed in a female hand. While you were engaged in picking up the other papers, and putting our friend to rights, I managed to obtain the name and the address of the sender. There is no call for you to appear so scandalised," he added. " I did not read the contents of the letter, merely the sender's address and her name. We will accordingly pay a call on Miss Deborah Hamilton at her home in Kensington this afternoon."

" And we will see what charmer has stolen our reverend friend's heart."

" Maybe, maybe. But first, let us attend to the inner man, then the spirit in the form of the concert, and to finish the day, we will satisfy our intellectual curiosity with our visit to Miss Hamilton. There is a kind of balance there, do you not think ? "

The afternoon's concert was more than something of a torment to me. My musical tastes never approached the degree of connoisseurship that was possessed by Sherlock Holmes, and tended more towards operetta. Though I could appreciate the technical virtuosity with which the maestro played his violin, I would have chosen a more

tuneful programme for my own pleasure, had I been presented with the opportunity. Holmes, for his part, appeared lost in a dreamy state, eyes closed, and one hand
gently beating time to the music. After the second encore,
which finished in a bravura display of a broken string and
horsehair flying from the performer's bow, we left the hall
and made our way to the street in Kensington where Miss
Deborah Hamilton resided.

The house was a handsome one, and had obviously been
repainted and decorated. " I wonder who this Miss Hamilton might be ? " I said to Holmes.

Holmes asked the maid who opened the door to us
whether Miss Hamilton was at home, presenting his card
to her. The answer came back shortly that she would be
delighted to see us, and we were ushered into the drawing-room of the house, where an elderly woman was sitting
in an armchair. The room itself was comfortably fur-
nished, and with bookshelves lining three of the four walls,
it spoke of the learning of its occupant.

" Forgive me for not rising," were Miss Hamilton's first
words to us, spoken in a soft cultivated voice. " My arth-
ritis is particularly virulent today. I was walking with a
friend last evening, and the cold and damp has aggravated
my condition."

" You are Miss Deborah Hamilton ? "

" That has always been my name." There was more than
a hint of humour in her reply.

" There is no other Deborah Hamilton living at this address ? " I could not help but ask. It was hard for me to
imagine that this elderly genteel lady could be the recipient of the Archdeacon's epistles of passion.

She looked at me strangely. " As far as I am aware, I
am the only person by this name living here," she said,

with a puzzled smile. " Have you any reason to believe otherwise ? "

I stammered some response, and moved to the chair, introducing myself, taking her small, yet firm and dry, hand.

" Of course I have heard of you, Mr. Holmes," she said to my friend. " And of you, too, Dr. Watson. Your accounts of the adventures you have shared together with Mr. Holmes have given me many hours of amusement."

It is always pleasant to hear praise for the fruits of one's labours with the pen, and I thanked her for her words.

" But what can I do for you two gentlemen ? " she asked. " I hardly believe that I have committed some crime of which I remain unaware." Her eyes fairly twinkled with good humour, and I was forced to smile at her words.

" Nothing as serious as that," Holmes laughed. " I simply wish to ask you if you are acquainted with the Venerable Harper-Barrington, the Archdeacon at Larrowby."

As these words, her demeanour, which up to this time had been friendly and open, changed markedly. " I do not see that it is any business of yours, Mr. Holmes, if no crime has been committed," she retorted. " He may or may not be known to me, but that is my affair, and not yours. Good afternoon to you gentlemen."

It was a definite dismissal, and we made quick apologies and left.

" She knows him, then ? " I said to Holmes once we were outside.

" Oh yes, she knows him well," he answered me. " I think we will take a trip up North. Go to King's Cross station and purchase two tickets for Larrowby. I will join you presently. Wait for me in the buffet."

I followed Holmes' instructions, but had not long to wait before he joined me, carrying a package bound up in brown paper. " You have the tickets ? Good, then let us be off."

The express train took us smoothly and easily to Larrowby station, whence we hired a cab to take us to the Cathedral Close, where the Archdeacon's lodging, a building in fine late medieval style, was located.

The Archdeacon himself answered the door, and was visibly staggered when he recognised Holmes and myself. " My dear sir ! " he exclaimed. " Though I did extend an invitation to you, I hardly expected you to take me up on it so soon. Do step in and take tea. A fresh pot can be easily arranged."

Once settled in the comfortable armchairs, Holmes enquired of our host, " As a matter of fact, it was not you with whom I wished to speak."

" Oh ? Then with whom ? "

" With Miss Kitty Bellecharme."

The effect on the elderly clergyman was electric. His face took on an expression of horror, and he came close to dropping his teacup, which he replaced on the saucer with trembling hands. " How ..? How in the world did you come to know of her ? "

" Through Miss Deborah Hamilton," Holmes smiled.

" She would never give me away ! " cried the Archdeacon.

" Nor did she," Holmes reassured him. " She maintained her silence. I have deduced the presence of Miss Bellecharme here from what I observed when we visited her."

" How much do you know ? "

" I believe I now know all," Holmes said calmly.

" But this is impossible," said the old man. " I thought that the existence of Miss Bellecharme was known only to Miss Hamilton and myself. I suppose now you will be demanding money from me to keep her existence a secret," he exclaimed indignantly.

To my astonishment, and that of the Archdeacon, Holmes threw back his head and laughed heartily. " My dear sir, I am not here to spread the word about Miss Bellecharme, and I would not take a penny from you to maintain her present state of discretion. I have only discovered her as a result of enquiries instigated at the request of your nephew, young Fairdale Hobbs."

A look of relief spread over the old man's face. " Forgive me, Mr. Holmes for my most un-Christian thoughts regarding your motives. For a while I was under the impression that you were of the same stamp as some of those other confounded private detectives of whom I have heard so much ill. So young Fairdale saw me last night in London and worried about me ? "

" After having discovered scraps of a letter from Miss Hamilton asking for more passion in Miss Bellecharme's work, and the corner of a manuscript of hers which had escaped the fire."

" I see. How careless of me," remarked the Archdeacon, smiling broadly.

By now I was completely confused. " Pray tell me," I enquired of both, " what is going on. Where is this Miss Kitty Bellecharme, for example ? "

At this, Holmes redoubled his laughter, joined by the clergyman.

" You are looking at him," admitted the latter, pausing for breath in his merriment. " I am Miss Kitty Bellecharme."

" And Miss Deborah Hamilton is her literary agent, and these," opening the parcel that he had brought from London, " are her collected works." The parcel proved to

contain a number of cheap novelettes, of the genre generally described as " romantic" and purchased by servants or
shop-girls for their entertainment. " I had hoped," continued Holmes, still smiling, " that Miss Bellecharme would
be able to sign her name in these."

" Well, well, Mr. Holmes, you are a man of surprises."

" How in the world," I interjected, " did you come to
these conclusions ? "

" Yes, I also shall be interested to know how you came to
discover all this," our host agreed. " I take it you two gentlemen will stay for dinner, and lodge with me tonight, by
the way ? It is a long way back to London, and dusk has
already fallen."

We accepted with gratitude, and Holmes, having received
permission to light his pipe, sat back and commenced his
narrative.

" From the description of the letter which had been sent
to Miss Kitty Bellecharme at the poste restante, I felt
that there was some element of subterfuge involved. Why
would our host here wish to keep letters addressed to a
woman who did not even possess an address ? But I still
wish to know why that phrase about requiring more passion was contained in the scrap of letter that your nephew
discovered ? "

The Archdeacon broke into loud guffaws. " Oh, my
goodness," he laughed. " Was that really the phrase he discovered ? My latest manuscript of ' Sally and the Earl of
Devonshire' was not altogether to Miss Hamilton's taste.
She required Sally and her noble lover to display a little
more intimacy—nothing distasteful, you understand—but
simply less Platonic, perhaps." He sat back, still smiling.
" Go on, Mr. Holmes, this is most amusing."

" Then there was the question of the burnt quires of

paper in the grate, which were definitely in your hand, according to your nephew, and of which only one corner survived, containing a most suggestive phrase." He reached in his pocket and produced the document in question, which he handed over, to the initial astonishment, followed by the laughter, of the author.

" Well, bless my soul ! No wonder he thought I was carrying on some sort of dalliance. And then he saw me in Piccadilly on one of my unannounced visits to London with Miss Hamilton. But surely he would have realised that any kind of liaison with a lady of her years was unlikely ? "

" It was a foggy evening, and apparently the lady had muffled her face against the damp."

" Ah yes, I remember. What a comedy of errors this is turning out to be ! And how did you come to know of Miss Hamilton ? "

" Ah, that was from a letter that you were carrying when you collided with Dr. Watson here outside the Carlton. I picked it up and could not help but remark the sender's name and address."

" Hardly gentlemanly of you," the Archdeacon reproved Holmes, but gently. " Considering that you yourself were on the trail of one whom you might reasonably have suspected of ungentlemanly conduct, perhaps you may be forgiven." His round face creased in a smile, and it was clear to me that he was enjoying this exposition of the discovery of his secrets.

" At the Club, I requested you to write on a piece of paper, and I was able to satisfy myself that both the paper and the writing matched those already in my possession."

" Why yes, I have frequently written my little oeuvres on the Club paper, and it was one of those drafts that found its way into the fireplace when young Fairdale surprised me that evening."

" And when we visited Miss Hamilton, it was obvious that she knew you, from her reaction to a mention of your name, and also that she was connected with the world of books and publishing. One whole shelf of her bookcases seemed to be devoted to the work of Miss Kitty Bellecharme."

Our host blushed. " I must confess that Miss Bellecharme has been most prolific. I discovered some thirty years ago that I had a talent for producing this kind of writing, and enjoyed the exercise. You can imagine that it produces a most pleasing contrast to the everyday life of a provincial archdeacon, though it is naturally not one that I wish to bring to the notice of my flock, or indeed of anyone. Miss Hamilton is a distant cousin of some kind, and I had heard that she acted as a literary agent who sold manuscripts to publishers on the behalf of authors. I contacted her under this ridiculous name of Kitty Bellecharme, giving a poste restante address, and much to my surprise, she accepted the book and sold it to a magazine as a serial. Since then, as you can see, I have had success in my other life." He gestured towards the pile of books that Holmes had brought with him. " It is most amusing. My housemaid appears to be a devotee of my work, being totally unaware that it is her master who is the author of the romances I have from time to time discovered her devouring."

" And at some stage in the proceedings Miss Hamilton discovered your true identity ? "

" I informed her myself, after some five years of doing business with her. She was surprised, as you can imagine, but we decided to leave the arrangements regarding

Miss Bellecharme and her postal arrangements unchanged, since they were working successfully."

" And the money that Hobbs has told us you donate to good causes ? "

" It is all Miss Bellecharme's doing. I have not profited one penny personally from this work."

Holmes sat back and puffed at his pipe, while I digested this tale.

At length, the Archdeacon broke the silence. " Do you think I should continue, Mr. Holmes, now that my secret is known ? "

" By all means, my dear sir. You are giving harmless pleasure to thousands, I dare say, and the money you are receiving and redistributing is undoubtedly doing good to many others. Furthermore, it is obvious from your account and your manner that it is an activity that gives you great pleasure. I would recommend, though, that you inform your nephew of these activities. He appears to be genuinely concerned about your moral well-being."

" I will do so. Now it is time for dinner, and I trust that tomorrow morning you will give me the pleasure of allowing me to escort you around some of our local churches to admire some of the architecture therein."

" If Miss Kitty Bellecharme and you can spare the time, we will be delighted to accompany you," Sherlock Holmes answered him, with a warm smile.

An Account of the
Victor Lynch Forgery

(as related by Inspector Charles
Lestrade of Scotland Yard)

Editor's Note

As I was looking in the dispatch-box, among the varied papers, not all of which appeared to concern themselves with Sherlock Holmes, my eye was caught by a long letter written in an unfamiliar crabbed hand, with the sender's address given as " Scotland Yard". Naturally this piqued my curiosity, and I picked up the sheaf of papers, and perused them with interest.

It transpired that the writer was one Charles Lestrade, whom we all know as the most famous of all of Sherlock Holmes' official contemporaries and colleagues. The letter started as one of condolence to Dr. Watson on the loss of his friend Sherlock Holmes following the tragic events at Meiringen, but as I read on, I was increasingly interested in the other case—the first one in which he collaborated with Holmes, at the beginning of the famous detective's career, and which he describes to Watson.

This is the case to which Holmes refers in A Study in Scarlet, when he says that " Lestrade is a well-known detective. He got himself into a fog recently over a forgery case, and that was what brought him here." The case is also referred to in The Sussex Vampire, where Holmes mentions the entry of " Victor Lynch, the forger" in his Index.

So here is Sherlock Holmes, before he became famous, and without Watson, as seen through a different pair of eyes to those with which we usually see him, and not always as sympathetic or as understanding as those of Watson. It is, however, notable for the grudging respect in which Lestrade undoubtedly holds Holmes, a respect which was not always apparent from the way in which he (Lestrade) was described by Watson. It is also notable for the way in which Lestrade recreates Holmes' distinctive manner of speech, which is more than likely the result of his police training.

Y DEAR DR. WATSON,
It was with a profound sense of loss and genuine grief that I read the letter that you were kind enough to send me from Switzerland. I offer my deepest and sincere condolences, knowing as I do the strong friendship and affection that obtained between you and Mr. Holmes. Naturally I will attend the service of memorial at the time and place you mentioned in your letter, and I am sure that Inspectors Gregson and Bradstreet, among others, will wish to attend and pay their respects to a man who has been of such great assistance to the police forces of this country.

As you know, I was acquainted with Mr. Holmes before you met him, at the time when he was living and carrying on his work from rooms in Montague Street. If you have no objection, I would like to take this opportunity of giving you some details of the case which brought him and me together for the first time. I have enjoyed your writing of the cases where Mr. Holmes and I worked together and you were present, and it struck me that it would make a pleasant addition to your work if this were to be " written up", as they say, in your literary style. You can guess that the nature of my work does not make for a smooth flow of words, and I know my masters in different areas when I meet them, whether it be story-telling, or even in my business of detection, where I freely admit that, by breaking the rules, Mr. Holmes often brought a fresh set of eyes and a new approach to the cases in which I was involved.

Let me tell you, then, of the story of the Lynch forgery case, which I hope will convince you that even though I may sometimes have appeared a little displeased with the methods and conclusions that Mr. Holmes employed, it was little more than a competitive urge, such as one sportsman may experience in a race against another. Please accept this as my tribute to a man who, for all his faults, displayed a greater understanding of the work of a detective than any other I have encountered.

With my deepest respects, I remain yours most sincerely,

[Signature]

C. Lestrade (Detective Inspector, Metropolitan Police)

T THE TIME I DESCRIBE, I had been newly promoted to the rank of Detective Inspector in the Criminal Investigation Department after more than five years' service with the police force. It was a good chance for me to display whatever abilities I may possess, and I took every chance I was given to do so. As you have probably noticed, there is often a good-natured rivalry between two officers in the force who are making their way up the ranks, and my particular rival was Tobias Gregson, one of the best officers in the London area. He has worked with you and Mr. Holmes on a number of occasions, of course, including that case when you and I first met, which you entitled " A Study In Scarlet".

However, the occasion on which I first came into contact with Mr. Holmes was a case of a problem with a will. An elderly gentleman by the name of Parkins had died some two months previously, and when his will was read, it was discovered that there was a codicil. According to this addition, which had been drawn up and witnessed some six months earlier, his sons, who had expected to inherit most, if not all, of his considerable fortune, were virtually cut out of the will, and most of the money was to go to a niece.

The sons, Reginald and Lionel by name, had questioned

the validity of the codicil, but it appeared to have been drawn up in a regular fashion by a solicitor, who was also acting as executor of the estate. There was a vague connection between my parents and the old man—my father had worked in the same firm alongside Mr. Parkins at one time before the latter's speculations on the Stock Exchange which had brought him his wealth. Because of this, the two brothers wished to consult me on the matter, knowing my occupation as a detective. I agreed to their request for a meeting, given the family connection, though I was unsure of what value I would be to them.

I met the two at a hotel in London, following their suggestion, and though I do not as a rule base my judgements on first impressions, especially those impressions which result from a man's personal appearance, I was not in any way well-disposed towards them. Both possessed what to my eyes was a shifty appearance, though both carried themselves and spoke as gentlemen.

" The point is, Lestrade," Lionel Parkins, the younger, said to me, " that though our father was generous in his way to us, and I don't want to speak ill of the dead here—"

" Particularly about our father," his older brother interrupted.

" Exactly," the other agreed. " The fact is that the governor, as we called him, never allowed us access to the cash in his bank account, telling us that it would be time enough for us to have it when he had gone before. Well, you see, he's gone, and we don't have the cash."

" And the devil of it is," broke in Reginald Parkins, " that we were expecting him to leave us the money at some time soon—of course, we were hoping he would remain with us for a long time, but I think you understand what I mean here—but both of us have borrowed against the expectation of the money coming to us, and now it seems that this wretched girl has taken it all."

" I am unsure as to what you want me to do to put things right," I said.

" My dear Lestrade," said the younger brother. " Surely you must see that the codicil is a forgery. Our father would never have made such an arrangement without letting us know about it."

I have in my time known of several parents who have cut their children out of their wills, unbeknown to their off-spring, but said nothing regarding this, choosing instead to turn the conversation elsewhere. " What do you know of this Miss Jenny Whitcombe ? " I asked.

" She may have been Miss Whitcombe when the codi-cil was written," said Lionel, " but she is now Mrs. Lynch. She was married to a Victor Lynch, a clerk in a provincial lawyer's office or some such, a few months before our fa-ther's death. Neither Reginald nor I has seen her since we were children, and she did not attend the governor's funer-al," he added with a sneer.

" To be fair," Reginald Parkins said, " it is almost cer-tain that she knew nothing of the codicil. However, she has made no response to our requests for a settlement."

I could think of no good reason why she should make a settlement, but held my peace on the matter. " How much was your father's estate worth ? "

" It is difficult to say until the house in Henley has been sold, but there was twenty thousand pounds in the bank, and about the same amount in securities."

" A goodly sum, then. You are not living in the house, then ? "

" No, we set up a bachelor establishment together some years ago. The governor lived quietly with a cook and a housekeeper, whom we have been given to understand have been paid off, preparatory to the house being sold. Mrs. Lynch lives some way out of Town, in Woking. I have her address here." He passed me a scrap of paper.

" Let me understand. You would like me to investigate this matter, and discover if there has been any underhand activity."

" Of course there has been underhand activity ! " exclaimed the older brother. " Is it not obvious ? We want you to bring this woman to trial. That's what you police fellows are there for, isn't it ? Naturally, there will be something in it for you when we receive our rightful inheritance."

" I fear you misunderstand the duties and the powers of a police officer," I informed them, as stiffly as I could manage. " Even if I had the time available to carry out an investigation such as you suggest, I would not be empowered to do so."

" Then hire one of these private detectives who seem to be appearing all over the place."

" Why can you not do that yourself ? " I asked.

" It would never do for us to be seen consorting with such a person," said Lionel Parkins. " We do have positions to maintain, you realise."

" Very good," I said, by now thoroughly irritated at the pretensions of these two, telling myself that I would drop the matter as soon as I left them. " I will let you know if I discover any such person who may meet with your approval. Good day to you both."

I walked back to my office at Scotland Yard, fuming at the manner in which I and my profession had been regarded. A young sergeant working with me, Stanley Hopkins, was waiting in my office.

" Yes, Sergeant," I said to him, after five minutes of silence had passed between us, during which time I had attended to some paperwork, I fear with a very bad grace. " I am out of sorts, and you are free to know the reason why."

I explained my recent encounter with the Parkins brothers, and how they had attempted to misuse the police force for their own purposes. " If I felt any better disposed towards them, I would indeed seek out a private detective."

" If you change your mind about that, Inspector," Hopkins said to me, " I can recommend the very man for your purposes. He is a young man, just down from University, though I believe he did not take his degree."

" What is he doing for a living ? Is he a private detective ? "

" He prefers the term 'consulting detective'. He has handled one or two affairs for friends with some success, I believe, but he is not the usual type that you and I run across."

" In what way is he different ? "

" He has the most extraordinary mind that I have ever encountered. He has the most amazing capacity for knowledge on all manner of out-of-the-way subjects, and he is able to link seemingly unconnected facts in an remarkable fashion. He also has a talent for observation which is unique in my experience."

" If he has all these talents, and he wishes to be a detective, surely he should join the Force ? "

Hopkins laughed at this. " If you had ever met Mr. Sherlock Holmes, for that is his name, you would not ask such a question. His habits and lack of regard for authority and correct conduct would ensure that he was thrown out of any official body immediately."

I was intrigued by this description. " How do you come to know him ? "

" I was walking past the British Museum one day, when I noticed a tall lanky fellow looking upwards. I stopped and followed the direction of his gaze, but could see nothing of interest, and remarked as much to him. Whereupon, he suggested, since I was a police officer, that I might be interested in the doings of the occupant of the top room in the house which he had been observing."

" You were in uniform ? " I asked.

" No, that is the extraordinary thing about it. I asked him how he had me marked as a police officer, and he gave me an answer which involved the way that I walked, and held myself, which to his eye, so he said, was unique to the officers of the Metropolitan Police."

" And the occupant of the room ? "

" I hailed a beat constable, and we made our way to the room, with this Holmes following us. We obtained permission from the landlord to break down the door, the room being seemingly unoccupied, and discovered a small printing press which had been creating five pound notes, of a somewhat inferior quality."

" This was the Ridgmount Gardens counterfeiting case, then ? "

" Yes, it was, sir."

" I never saw any mention of this Holmes in your report," I said.

Hopkins looked abashed. " He particularly wished his name not to be mentioned, sir. He told me that he did not wish to be associated with what he regarded as such a trivial matter, and he would be obliged if his part in it was withheld. He was perfectly polite about it, and presented me with his card."

It surprised me that man starting to make his way in a profession of this kind did not wish to take credit for his successes. " Did he tell you why he suspected the occupant to have committed a crime ? "

" Yes, he did. He told me that he had remarked the fire being lit in the room at odd times, as he could tell from the smoke emerging from the chimney. He appeared to be aware of which rooms were connected to each chimney, living, as he told me, in lodgings occupying a similar design of house. He had also marked the appearance on fine days of sheets of paper outside the window, seemingly drying."

" And his conclusions ? "

" That the fire was needed to dry some material on wet days, and he concluded that they were these sheets of paper that appeared on fine days. From what he could see, the sheets were blank, but he had noticed water dripping from them, meaning to his mind that a watermark was being applied to them."

" And from that, he assumed that an act of counterfeiting was in progress ? "

" He admitted to me that he had followed the inhabitant of the room to an artists' supplier, where he had purchased a number of fine burins such as are used to engrave copper plates. That, in his view, clinched the matter. Following this case, I confess that I have occasionally met Mr. Holmes, and sought his opinion on a number of puzzling details. In every instance, his guesses have been proven correct by the facts. The extraordinary thing is that he seems to seek no reward, or even credit, for this assistance, declaring that the solution of the problem is itself a reward in his eyes."

" Well, well," I answered. " You should introduce me to this remarkable person."

My feelings regarding this matter were such that

although I had no particular wish to assist the Parkins
brothers, at the very least the facts of which I had been informed allowed me to consider the possibility that a crime
of some kind had been committed. While I had no official
permission to investigate the matter, it seemed to me that
the employment of an amateur—one who was not involved
in the business of detection simply for financial gain—
would at one stroke both fulfil any possible obligations to
the Parkins family and satisfy my professional curiosity.

Accordingly, Hopkins arranged for himself and me to
meet Sherlock Holmes in a Bloomsbury restaurant.

" This is Mr. Lestrade, my friend," Hopkins introduced
me to the thin-faced man who was awaiting our arrival at
the restaurant table, idly making notes in a memorandum
book. I had specifically requested that Hopkins not mention my occupation, instructing him that I was to be introduced merely as one seeking his assistance on a matter
concerning a friend's inheritance.

" The rank is Inspector, is it not ? " were Sherlock
Holmes' first words to me, as he rose to his feet, towering
over me, and shook my hand warmly.

" You have been talking to Mr. Holmes about me," I accused Hopkins, somewhat annoyed. I had hoped that I
could have avoided being identified as a police officer.

" Calm yourself. He has done no such thing," remarked
the amateur detective. " It was obvious from your manner of walking, and from the way that you observed and
took in your surroundings as you walked into the restaurant just now, that you are a policeman. I would venture
to suggest, without any attempt at flattery, that you are
more than proficient in your profession, and when I likewise observe a certain deference towards you from Sergeant

Hopkins here, I assume that you are his superior in the force. Hence it is Inspector Lestrade, is it not ? "

Of course now you and I, Doctor, became used to these little tricks that Mr. Holmes used to play. But this was the first time that I had encountered him, and his methods, and I was forced to chuckle at his words. " Correct, Mr. Holmes. What else can you tell me about myself ? "

He looked me over with what I can only describe as a critical eye. " You are left-handed, as is obvious from the merest glance. You have been in the Army, almost certainly as a sergeant in the sappers, and you served overseas, probably in India. So much is obvious from your overall bearing, your stature, and you bear the marks of having suffered some tropical disease. Among other interesting facts that I may remark about you, I would observe that you are at present unmarried, but hope to change that at some time in the near future. You have also, if you will permit me to remark the fact, recently consumed a boiled egg, some fragments of the shell of which are still adhering to your waistcoat."

I looked down at the offending garment, and brushed away the fragments of my breakfast which were still unfortunately present. I could not help but laugh. " Truly remarkable," I said to him. " All that you have told me is gospel truth. I suffered from the cholera while I served with the sappers in Madras, and I was lucky to escape with my life from that dreadful disease. On one point, however, you are slightly at fault. The rank that I held when I was discharged was merely that of corporal."

" Well, I cannot expect to be always correct. I flatter myself that I have a certain talent in this field, but I am as yet a beginner in the science of detection."

" You regard it as a science, then ? "

" Indeed I do. How do you, as a professional, regard it ? "

" It is a matter of painstaking method and hard work. I hardly think that my superiors would find it worthwhile for me to engage in flights of speculative fancy."

" Well, we may agree to disagree on this matter," he said. " I believe you wish to consult me on some affair. May I enquire whether this is a police case ? "

I gave him the details of the situation, and he listened to me in silence, his fingertips pressed together in a way that I came to know well over the years. At the end of my recital of the facts he spoke.

" I take it that you have made no investigations of your own so far ? You have not, for example, examined the document in question—that is to say, the codicil ? " I shook my head. " Or visited the dead man's house, which is currently unoccupied, according to your account ? No ? Then I shall make it my business to do so."

" Before you proceed further with this matter," I interrupted, " it will be necessary for me to know what fee you expect to charge for your services."

His response to my query was a smile. " My dear Inspector, I am at present learning my trade. It would be singularly inappropriate for an apprentice to demand financial recompense from a master."

You may imagine that I was relieved to hear these words. As Mr. Holmes had deduced, though to this day I am still unsure as to how exactly he had arrived at that conclusion, I was engaged to be married, and money was at that time a matter of some concern to me. Although the Parkins brothers had promised me a share of whatever legacy could be obtained as the result of my efforts, I was not convinced that any such money would be forthcoming.

The rest of this, my first encounter with Sherlock Holmes, was taken up with providing him with the details of the case as I understood them. At the end of the meeting, he stood up, shook my hand, and assured me that he would let me know of any developments in the case within the next few days.

In the event, I received a telegram at my office in the Yard the next afternoon.

" Meet me tonight at 8 same restaurant. S. Holmes."

No doubt you, Doctor, have become accustomed over the years to our late friend's impetuous methods of communication. At that time, however, I was unaware of Sherlock Holmes' predilection for telegrams, and I therefore assumed that this was a matter of extreme urgency and importance.

I arrived at the restaurant some ten minutes before the appointed hour, and precisely on the stroke of eight, Sherlock Holmes strode into the restaurant and seated himself at the table.

" I trust that you are free to accompany me tomorrow morning," were his first words to me. " I wish to examine the house of the dead man. Be at Waterloo station at 10 o'clock, and we will make our way to Parkins' house in Henley together."

I was completely taken aback by this request, as well as the abrupt manner in which it was made. " You cannot expect me to drop my current work and accompany you simply because you wish it," I said to him. " You may not be aware, not being a police officer yourself, of the amount of work that accumulates on my desk and the responsibilities that accompany it."

" Not even if it is in the interests of investigating a possible crime ? " he answered me.

" What in the world do you mean by that ? "

" I believe there has been some wrongdoing, but as yet I am unsure as to exactly what crime, if any, has actually been committed, let alone the perpetrator. However, I am reasonably certain that some of the answers lie in the dead man's house in Henley. I have no right to request entry as a private citizen, but the presence of a police inspector from Scotland Yard should open doors which would otherwise remain locked to me."

" Of course, if it is a question of a crime that has been committed, I will be ready to assist you. But I warn you, I will not have my time wasted on what may turn out to be a fruitless chase."

" I can promise you that it will not be completely fruitless, though I can make no promises as to the nature of our quarry. I have already travelled to Woking, and in the guise of an employee of the deceased's bank, made discreet enquiries of Mrs. Lynch as to the relationship between her and her late uncle."

" Well, there are some things that you can do as an amateur which are forbidden to us professionals, I suppose. And the result of your enquiries ? "

" I discovered that the lady in question had a vague memory of meeting her uncle some twenty years ago when she was aged about five. Since then, all exchanges between them had been restricted to an exchange of greetings at Christmas time. It therefore seems extremely unlikely to me that Parkins would suddenly have changed his will in her favour unless the two sons had performed some action which would have brought them into disfavour with their father."

" It is not for me to speak ill of others," I said, " but I would not give two pennies for their good conduct. In my limited experience of such matters, though, it seems to me that the individual who is cutting another out of his will usually ascribes a reason for the action."

" No such reason was given, according to Mrs. Lynch, who informed me of the details of the codicil. She would seem to have an excellent memory on the subject, and there was no reason for me to suspect that she was telling me anything other than the truth. According to her recollection, the codicil appears to have been drawn up and signed and witnessed in exactly the same way as the will. Even the witnesses appeared to be the same, according to her recollection—maybe the clerks of the solicitor's office which drew up the will. If it does turn out to be a forgery, I have no doubt that it will prove to be a very sophisticated one, which I do not believe it will be easy to prove. She did, however, mention some differences between the signature of the dead man on the will and that on the codicil. Based on her observations, I have some suspicions, which can be most easily answered by reference to the dead man's house. Hence my request to you to accompany me on my quest."

Despite myself, Mr. Holmes' words interested me. What he was proposing would make a welcome change from my everyday routine of petty crime, and drunken assaults by unknown assailants. " I will be with you," I answered him. " How do you propose to gain access to the house ? "

" Mrs. Lynch was good enough to provide me with the name of the agents who are in charge of the house, pending its disposal. She and her husband have no intention of living there, and propose to sell it as soon as practicable. I was assured by her that the contents of the house are still in place, and to the best of her knowledge, have remained almost untouched since the day that Parkins died."

" So you wish me to use my official position to allow you to enter the house ? "

" Quite simply, yes. You have put it in a nutshell. I am confident that a few minutes' examination of the furnishings of the house will reveal the relevant facts to me. Then it is agreed, we meet at Waterloo station tomorrow morning and travel to Henley together ? "

You may think it strange that I as an experienced officer of the law was agreeing to an action which, if not altogether illegal, certainly stretched the bounds of what was possible for me to do in my official capacity. The truth is that even after such a short period of acquaintance Sherlock Holmes impressed me in the degree of his self-confidence in a fashion that no other man has been able to do, before or since. I was so intrigued by his cocksure attitude, that I was almost forced to agree, simply in order to satisfy my curiosity.

For the remainder of the meal, for which he insisted on paying, we talked on a variety of subjects, and I was astounded by the breadth and depth of his knowledge of criminal affairs.

" I am glad that you never considered taking up a criminal career," I laughed at one point in our conversation.

" Why do you assume that I never did so ? " he answered me. " When I first discovered for myself that I possessed this analytical faculty, and the ability to deduce causes from effects, I realised that these were powers which were not given to everybody, and I must confess to you that for a short period I considered using them for my personal gain, whether or not such actions fell inside the law. It would have pleased my vanity to be the man whom Scotland Yard sought in vain. Do not raise your eyebrows in that way, my dear Inspector. I know full well, and so do you, that the majority of criminals are hopeless bunglers, and that however hard they try to escape you, you will always catch them in the end. If I had taken up a criminal career, believe me, you might not even be aware that a crime had been committed, let alone be able to identify and entrap the criminal." He laughed, and refilled my glass with a remarkably fine Moselle wine.

" It would be interesting to take you up on that challenge someday," I thought to myself, but did not say aloud.

The next morning saw us—that is, Mr. Holmes and myself—travelling to Henley, where, by dint of showing the papers identifying me as a police officer, we were able to gain entrance to the house previously occupied by the late Mr. Parkins. As you might expect from a house which had not been occupied for a number of months, dust was everywhere, but the furnishings all appeared to be in place. The first room we entered seemed to be a study or a library, with books lining the walls. To my surprise, my companion pulled out a magnifying lens from the pocket of his overcoat and proceeded to examine the tops of the books and the shelves.

" Mark this well, Inspector," he said. " The shelves were obviously dusted regularly while Parkins was alive, but the books were not touched. These books have remained untouched in the shelves for a number of years, I would say. And look here." A row of directories stood on one of the shelves, containing a volume for each year, starting some twenty years previously. The sequence came to an abrupt end three years before the date of which I am writing. He then pointed to another set of volumes, also ceasing at the same date. Between us we counted five sets of annual directories, each of which ended at the same year. " Curious, very curious," he muttered, almost to himself, as he turned his attention to the desk.

" Here is a scrapbook," he showed me, " in which it appears that Parkins used to paste clippings from newspapers describing any subject that took his fancy. See, here is a clipping from the *Daily Telegraph* about the sighting of sea-serpents in Sumatra—"

" How do you know this is from the *Daily Telegraph* ? " I asked him.

" The type, man, the type. You would not mistake a bulldog for a terrier, I take it, though they are both dogs ? The founts and styles in which newspapers are set differ more from each other than do breeds of dogs. Believe me, I am of the opinion that a thorough knowledge of type and papers is as necessary to a detective as any other branch of knowledge. But no matter. Look here, each article is dated in what can only be Parkins' own hand." He turned to the end of the book. " These entries cease about three years ago. And compare the writing of the last entries with those of earlier clippings."

" The writing is larger and more untidy towards the end. He has even written over the clippings themselves in one or two places."

" Precisely. And what does that tell you ? "

" I have no idea. What does it tell you, Mr. Holmes ? Is this relevant ? "

" I would say that it is vital, at least as far as the business in which we are currently involved is concerned. It tells me that we will find a large loupe in the drawers of the desk here." He opened the central drawer of the desk, and triumphantly produced a fine example of a magnifying lens, as he had predicted. " Now do you understand ? "

I had no idea what he meant by this.

" Never mind. Maybe a visit to the bedroom will make things clearer." We went upstairs, and soon discovered the room which had obviously been used as Parkins' bedroom. Mr. Holmes pointed out to me that gas had not been laid on to the house, and that it had been lit by oil lamps and candles. I examined the candle beside the bed, and noted that it had never been lit.

" That is to be expected," said Mr. Holmes when I re-marked the fact. " Examine the wick of the oil lamp on the dressing-table."

I did as he asked, and discovered that it too had never been lit, judging by its appearance. " You expected that, also ? " I asked.

" Indeed I did. Now examine the washstand. Where are Parkins' razor, shaving soap and brush ? "

" They are missing. You will tell me that this, too, was expected ? "

" Of course I expected this."

" But I am still puzzled." It was now apparent that Sherlock Holmes was following some train of thought that remained hidden to me.

" Well, well. I am sure that you will come to the correct conclusion in time."

Mr. Holmes had now brought to my notice several items which he undoubtedly considered to be of significance. I had failed to grasp their meaning, but in my defence, I would say to my knowledge there was no detective in the Yard who would have done so. Even so, I was irritated by the air of superiority that Mr. Holmes was displaying.

" And now that we have seen all that there is to see here, we should pay a call on Ellis and Trumbull, the firm of solicitors in Maidenhead who were responsible for drawing up the will and the codicil."

" You believe there to be something strange in the matter of the codicil ? "

" I know what I think we shall find when we come to examine the original documents. Let us be off now."

As you know, Doctor, when Mr. Holmes was in one of these moods, there was no holding him back. At that time I did not know this, and I attempted to persuade him to carry out the errand on another day, but he was not to be restrained by me.

We soon found ourselves in the office of Henry Ellis, the senior partner of the firm. I had no idea as to what the forthcoming line of enquiry might be, so I sat silently, but ready to stop the proceedings should Mr. Holmes step across the line of the law.

He began by introducing the object of his enquiry, and asking if the documents in question—that is to say, the will and codicil—were available for inspection.

" I fail to see why you should not see them," said the solicitor, calling for a clerk to retrieve the documents and bring them to us.

Once they had been spread out on the table, we examined them closely.

" They appear to have been written in the same hand," I said.

" I believe that is the case," Ellis answered. " One of our clerks is usually responsible for the actual preparation of the documents, though of course I or Mr. Trumbull will be responsible for the wording and the terms and conditions in almost every case."

" In almost every case ? " asked Sherlock Holmes

" There may be a few occasions when a clerk will handle these matters."

" This will, for instance ? "

" The will was definitely drawn up by me some years ago—you may see the date here. I distinctly remember going to Mr. Parkins' house and discussing the matter with him in his study. Following that discussion, I returned here with my notes, asked one of the clerks to write it out, and then take the draft, which I had checked, to the client's house for signing."

" He did not come here ? "

" He was an elderly gentleman, and we had done a considerable amount of business for him in the past. It would have been churlish for us to have insisted that he visit us."

" So you did not see him sign the will himself ? "

" No, but that would in no way invalidate it, if that is what you are implying." The solicitor seemed to be more than a little irritated by Holmes' line of questioning, and I confess that I also found it to be a little harsh.

" I was not for a moment suggesting anything of the kind. I am merely attempting to ascertain the facts of the case. So the clerk wrote it and was responsible for its being signed and properly witnessed ? "

" That is correct."

" The witnesses being ? "

" The housekeeper and the butler at Mr. Parkins' establishment. I have no reason to believe that they have any suspicion of dishonesty attached to them."

It appeared to me that Ellis was uncomfortable in his answers, to my mind hiding something that he would sooner have left hidden, and this suspicion was soon confirmed as Mr. Holmes pursued his line of questioning, which I

freely admit was producing the facts we required in a most
efficient manner.

" May we now turn to the codicil ? I see that it is written in the same hand as the will."

" Quite possibly. Yes, now that I come to think of it, the
same clerk was responsible for writing out both the will
and the codicil."

" What were your thoughts when Mr. Parkins informed
you of the contents of the codicil ? "

At this point, the solicitor became red in the face, and
mopped his brow with a handkerchief. " Mr.—"

" Holmes," I reminded him.

" Thank you. Mr. Holmes, I have to tell you that the
first time that I set eyes on that codicil was when I read it
following Mr. Parkins' death. And I must tell you that it
came as a big surprise to me. But it appeared to be properly signed, and in a proper legal form. I questioned the two
witnesses, I may add, and they both confirmed that they
had witnessed their master signing the paper, and had duly
marked the fact with their own signatures. Whether or not
I agreed with the disposition of the estate was immaterial—I was bound by the wishes of the dead man, expressed
in a legally binding document. And that is what I said
to the deceased's two scapegrace sons when they confront-
ed me and attempted to persuade me to change the law in
their favour."

" Then you were not responsible for drawing up this
document ? "

" No, this was carried out by the clerk who had previously written out the will, as you observed just now. I dispatched him to Mr. Parkins following our client's request
for a codicil. I felt that since he was already acquainted with the details of the will, as well as being known

to Parkins personally, it would be a relatively straight-forward task, and would provide the clerk with valuable experience."

" So you never saw it before the reading of the will ? "

" On my honour, Mr. Holmes, although we were named as the executors, and though we held the will and the codicil here at our offices, I never looked at it. Remiss of me, perhaps, but I do not think I have broken the law as a result of this omission."

" Neither do I. Inspector ? " Sherlock Holmes appealed to me. I shook my head. " But I would like to ask you, what would your reaction have been had you read this codicil before Parkins' death ? "

" I would have questioned it. Most certainly I would have questioned it and referred it back to our client. Such a radical step, involving such a large sum of money, would almost certainly have warranted some sort of explanation."

" Maybe it is time we had a word with this clerk. With your permission, sir ? "

The other shook his head in sorry. " I fear he is no longer with us. He left our employ some three months ago to marry. I can no doubt discover his current address. In Woking, I believe."

" And his name was Lynch ? " Holmes asked.

" Why, yes ! You know the man ? "

" I believe I do," said Sherlock Holmes. It seemed to me that he was smiling faintly as he said this. " Come, Inspector, I think it is time we went to Woking. Thank you for your help, Mr. Ellis. I believe I will be able to locate this Lynch with little trouble."

As we walked to the station, I could not help asking Sherlock Holmes about his conclusions.

" I do not understand it," I said to him. " What have you seen that I have not seen that leads you to Woking ? "

" You have seen all that I have seen," he told me. " What you have failed to do is to observe closely and draw the appropriate conclusions from the facts before your eyes. You saw the two papers, the will and the codicil, just now. What differentiated them ? "

" Little, as far as I could see, save for old Parkins' signature, which was more untidy and less well placed on the codicil than it was on the will."

" And that says nothing to you ? " Sherlock Holmes shook his head, and we proceeded in silence. I racked my brain in a vain attempt to work out for myself what he had deduced from what we had witnessed.

We arrived at Woking, and made our way to the house which Holmes had visited previously, the abode of Mr. and Mrs. Lynch. On ringing the bell, the housemaid assured us that Mrs. Lynch was not at home, and that " the master" was likewise absent, but was expected home shortly.

" In which case, please give him my card," said Sherlock Holmes, " and inform him that we intend calling in the next hour or so."

I hoped to gain some insight from Sherlock Holmes regarding the case, and I therefore proposed that we walk in the Park. In my experience, most men tend to speak more freely when walking, and I was pleased to find that this was also the case with Sherlock Holmes. As we walked, he explained to me what he had discovered.

" What do you make of the fact that the annual directories ceased to be collected three years ago, that the scrapbook likewise finished about the same time, that the lamp and candle we discovered in the bedroom remained unlit, and that the signature on the codicil was ill-formed and misplaced on the page ? "

" Absent-mindedness ? Old age ? " I said.

" Is it not obvious to you ? Old Parkins was blind by the time he had reached the end of his life. He had no need for candles or lamps, his hobby of his scrapbook came to an end, he had no need of the directories to which he had previously subscribed. Furthermore, and this is what is germane to our case here, he was unable to see where to sign the codicil."

I considered this. " If he could not see where to sign, he could never have read it," I said.

" Precisely. Let me reconstruct the events for you. This Victor Lynch worked in the Henley solicitor's office as a clerk. He became friendly with Parkins' niece, Jenny Whitcombe. Whether he knew of the relationship between her and Parkins before the acquaintanceship commenced, or whether he discovered this after he met her is immaterial to the actual facts of the matter, though if the former, his conduct becomes more reprehensible. In any event, he knew that he was about to marry into the family of one of his employer's wealthiest clients. Somehow, at least a portion of that elderly relative's money could well be his, were he to marry the girl. But first, he must ensure that the money would indeed go to him—or rather, to her, which amounts to much the same thing.

" He had met Parkins previously on the occasion that the will was drawn up, and it was a stroke of luck for him that Parkins wished to change the terms of his estate, and a further stroke of luck that his lazy superior sent him alone on the errand to Parkins' house. Maybe this was not an act that had been premeditated, but the idea possibly struck him as he sat there in the house talking to the

blind man, and he suddenly realised that Parkins' afflic-
tion could be turned to his own advantage."

" You mean that Parkins believed he was dictating a codicil, but whatever he dictated was ignored, and Lynch simply wrote down that his future bride was to inherit ? "

" Precisely. He was familiar, after all, with the original
will, having written it out, and was well-placed to produce
a valid codicil. We will probably never know what Parkins intended the codicil to express, unless Lynch choos-
es to tell us. Following the completion of the false codicil,
Lynch carefully guided the blind man's hand to the place
on the page—you noticed several drops of ink and a few
lines where the pen had initially been placed in the wrong
position, did you not ? And the faithful servants witnessed
the signature."

" It is a most infamous crime ! " I exclaimed.

" Indeed it is infamous, but it would be impossible to
prove the crime. If we confront Lynch with our findings,"
(and here may I add, Doctor, that I was touched, as I was
to be touched many times in the future, by Sherlock Holmes' sharing of the credit in the case) " he will undoubtedly
deny the accusation, and who is to gainsay him ? We lack
proof, and I believe that proof will never be forthcoming."
He broke off and pulled out his watch. " Let us return to
the Lynch residence. He should be returned by now."

The door was opened, and we were admitted to a weep-
ing Mrs. Lynch. Through her sobs she showed us a brief
note from her husband, informing her that he had left her,
and he had withdrawn their savings from their bank, but
she was not to worry, since he had left enough for her to
live on.

We visited the bank into which Mrs. Lynch told us the
inheritance from Parkins had been deposited, and learned

from the manager that Lynch had entered the bank just before closing time and had withdrawn all his money in five-pound Bank of England notes. He had also, as we had previously been informed, left a small sum which would earn his wife a relative pittance in interest.

Mr. Holmes and I assumed that he had received a message from some source—maybe another clerk at the solicitor's, though all the clerks denied it when I questioned them later—and had fled the coop. My first instinct was to find the man and bring him to justice, but Mr. Holmes disagreed with me.

" Even if you do manage to locate him, on what charge will you detain him ? "

" Why, on that of fraud, of course."

" And how will you prove this ? As I said to you earlier, there is one living witness—the suspect himself. No jury will ever convict him based on our deductions. You now realise, I trust, the importance of seeing trifles, but to persuade a jury of their significance..." He shrugged. " I believe Victor Lynch has achieved a status that many more experienced criminals would envy—that of being known to have committed a crime against which any attempts at prosecution are doomed to failure."

I saw the truth of Mr. Holmes' observation that it would be impossible to bring a successful prosecution, and accordingly decided not to proceed further with the investigation, though all my instincts and sense of justice rebelled at this. Lynch, it is hardly necessary for me to add, was never seen again, at least under that name.

I confess, though, that I experienced some satisfaction in watching the Parkins brothers' faces when I told them that the money they were expecting was now outside their grasp, and would remain for ever so.

ND THAT, DR. WATSON, is how I came to meet Mr. Sherlock Holmes, and the first case in which I witnessed his extraordinary powers, the likes of which I believe we will never again see. His death is a tragic loss to me, both professionally and personally, and even the removal of Professor Moriarty from the face of the earth is a poor exchange.

OTHER BOOKS FROM INKNBEANS PRESS

THE DEED BOX OF JOHN H. WATSON MD: HUGH ASHTON

 ONG thought lost, the box containing the untold tales of the great detective Sherlock Holmes, deposited in the vaults of Cox & Co. of Charing Cross so long ago, has recently come to light.

It was presented to Hugh Ashton of Kamakura, Japan, the maiden name of whose grandmother was Watson. Ashton has transcribed and edited the adventures he discovered in there, and they have been published by Inknbeans Press.

Eleven adventures from the Deed Box series, 360 6"x9" pages reproduced in the style of the original canonical adventures, and bound together for the first time as a hardcover volume.

These adventures of Sherlock Holmes are approved by The Conan Doyle Estate Ltd.

THE BRASS MONKEY:
SUSAN WELLS BENNETT

 DIGITAL BOXED SET of all four of the Brass Monkey novels: *Wild Life, Charmed Life, Night Life* and *New Life*.

Sun City, Arizona: where old people go to die.

At least that's what Milo, a retired border patrolman, thinks when he first arrives in the palm- and orange-tree-lined retirement community. He takes up photography to wile away his remaining days.

Before long, he is fighting and flirting with Claire, a young widow who is working through her trauma while volunteering at the zoo. He meets Sax, a former cop and the bartender at the Brass Monkey, and Sax's favorite barfly, Sondra.

Unable to turn off their suspicious natures, Milo and Sax see danger and intrigue simmering just beneath the serene picture-postcard settings of Arizona. And life will never be the same for any of them!

THE NICK WEST TRILOGY:
JIM BURKETT

COLLECTION of excitement, terror, heroes, villains, betrayal, revenge, government duplicity, madmen, chemical weapons, old scores, new vengeance, and lies exposed all under one cover.

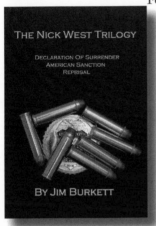Former DHS agent Nick West uses his skills with reasoning, and weaponry to stop an international cartel from selling United States to the highest bidder in *Declaration of Surrender*, a madman from selling a weapon of mass destruction so cruel and so indiscriminate even the governments vying to purchase it have second thoughts in *American Sanction*, and a killer out to avenge the death of someone who didn't deserve to die, and doesn't care who gets killed in the process in *Reprisal*.

INKNBEANS PRESS

 NKNBEANS PRESS is all about the ultimate reading experience. We believe books are the greatest treasures of mankind. In them are held all the history, fantasy, hope and horror of humanity. We can experience the past, dream of the future, understand how everything works from an atomic clock to the human heart. We can explore our souls, fight epic battles, swoon in love. We can fly, we can run, we can cross mighty oceans and endless universes. We can invite ancient cultures into our living room, and walk on the moon. And if we can do it with a decent cup of coffee beside us...well, what more can we ask, right?

Visit the Web site at www.inknbeans.com

Fresh Books Brewed Daily

Made in the USA
San Bernardino, CA
01 December 2013